# Dreamt

S. William Bennett

Dreamt

*Dedicated to the memory of*

**John Holland**

*and*

**William King**

*Even if only in name.*

Dreamt

## Table of Contents

Dreamt

# Dreamt

## Author's Note

This novel is set in early 19<sup>th</sup> century England, a place and time where sexism, racism, and a general prejudice regarding the superiority of one religion, were nearly universal attitudes.  Absolute intolerance for anyone deviating from a very narrowly defined model of sexuality was also commonplace.  Furthermore, gender was viewed as strictly binary and gender neutrality, for the most part, did not exist.

The characters in this book are depicted as people of their time.  Therefore, even the heroes of the story may sometimes behave in ways that would offend 21<sup>st</sup> century views to correctness.  Additionally, some outdated words that might be viewed as mildly offensive in the modern day will be used in the interest of providing a reasonably accurate depiction of the time and place.  While I choose to make my characters very progressive in most ways, I leave them endowed with a few noticeable vestiges of old and now odious biases as a reminder of the commonly held views of the society of which they are members.  Occasionally, a prejudiced view may be put forward as a means of describing the character's reckoning with, and often expunging of, such a view.  Notwithstanding, I have decided to write this story, and its characters, from the point of view of a male-centered culture.  This is in keeping with the period (and very greatly at odds with my personal instincts.)  Any antiquated attitudes appearing in this novel belong to the characters, and not to the author.

Sections referring to law enforcement and legal procedures are inspired by historical practices, but certainly deviate from these in some ways.  This is done in order to present a version of these institutions that is more accessible to modern readers, and that is perhaps just a small bit more dramatic.  Furthermore, reference materials pertaining to actual practices of the era are scarce, and often conflicting.  There would be some inaccuracies anyway, so they may as well enhance readability.

This work is inspired by a specific historical event, yet the narrative is entirely fictional.  It does refer to some historical individuals by their actual names.  I do not make any claim that the historical individuals mentioned herein actually took part in events resembling those described.  Except for a single event in this book (as discussed in the Afterword), any dates stated are arbitrary.

# Chapter 1 – Walter and Albert

In a continuation of a conversation already well underway, Walter Boniface asked his companion, "Did you know that the word, *'Dreamt'* is the only word in the English language that ends in the letters, '*M*', '*T*'?"

"Fascinating," replied Albert Medhurst, insincerely. "That fact was heretofore undreamt of."

The pale light from a flickering fire, augmented by a single beeswax candle, provided sufficient illumination for one to see, (if one were watching), that two gentlemen sat engaged in conversation in a small parlour. It did not, however, illuminate the room sufficiently to observe the subtle look of frustration that came over Mr. Boniface's face at that moment. "Don't be pedantic, Albert," he suggested. The conversation then proceeded in new directions.

By way of profession, Walter Boniface worked as a dealer in both rare and commonplace books. His bookshop was a small but well-stocked business. It was located in a reasonably well-to-do neighbourhood of Westminster, that borough being but one part of the great conglomeration of humanity straddling the River Thames, and collectively referred to as *London*. Some hours after the shop had closed for the day, he and his junior partner, Albert Medhurst, were enjoying a glass or three of gin in the former's rooms above the business, as they did on many evenings.

The date on which this conversation was taking place fell in the earlier part of the 19th century, although late enough in that century to have seen Napoleon safely ensconced on St. Helena. Was he still alive? Neither Mr. Boniface nor Mr. Medhurst had read anything to the contrary, so they assumed that he was, but they could not be sure. News of

deposed French emperors was not of primary concern to either gentleman.

Walter's female servant entered the room to tend the fire.  After she
added a log and raked the coals, Mr. Boniface said to her, "Thank you,
Mrs. Hewitt.  That will be all for tonight."

"Good night Mr. Boniface, Mr. Medhurst," she replied politely, and retired to her room.

"Albert," said the senior bookseller, getting back to business, "I had an
enquiry this afternoon from a gentleman searching for a copy of *L'Elogie
de la Folie* by Erasmus.  Would you make enquiries in the morning?  He
seems ardent in his desire for this volume and might pay a premium."

"A book written in Latin by a Dutchman, then translated into French.
That should indeed command a premium in London."  The junior partner stood and picked up the single candle that burned on a small table
between them.  He walked over to a side table and made use of a quill
and ink located thereupon to scribble a brief note on a scrap of brown
paper.  "Better write it down.  Can't remember a damn thing, you
know."  That task being done, and being already upon his feet, he retrieved the bottle of gin from the sideboard and proceeded to fill both
his glass and that of his close friend.

Having been distracted in thought, Walter did not notice his glass being
filled until the deed was done and the bottle removed.  "Oh... I might
not have taken any more drink tonight.  Very well.  We mustn't waste
good gin."  With that, he raised the glass to his lips.

"It will help you to sleep," observed Albert.

"Sleep, perhaps, but not to dream.  Gin muddles the dreams."

"Muddles the dreams, Walter?  That's rich!  Dreams are nothing but a
muddle from the start.  I think I could do very well without them."

"Oh, I must disagree, Albert," observed Walter Boniface. "Dreams are indeed confusing, yet I think that their understanding may shed light on many unsolved mysteries. I don't mean to say that the dreams themselves act as any portent of future trials or triumphs, but I think that in their reflection, we may learn something about the mind of civilized man. In the last several months, I have devoted considerable thought to my dreams, and I've found this to be a most worthwhile pursuit."

"You say, Walter, that dreams reveal to us the minds of civilized man. Do not savages dream as well?"

"I doubt not that all men experience dreams as strange and bizarre as our own, although perhaps with less complexity and symbolism. Our lives are very much removed from the natural environment, whereas the person that many Englishmen might call a *'savage'* exists today much as his ancestors have lived for countless generations. He lives close to the natural environment where change is slow. His mind is less challenged by continual progress, or at least those things that we tend to call progress. He has experienced fewer unexpected and unnatural stimuli. Therefore, surely, he cannot develop the complexity of dreams that we might."

"And what of women?" Albert asked. "Do men alone dream with great complexity or do women share in that skill as well?"

After a very few moments of thought, Walter responded, "I think women must surely dream with as great complexity as do we, Albert. Women, especially ladies of society, might be said to live lives even further removed from the natural environment than do most men. I don't doubt that their dreams are as intricate as our own, even if the subject matter is more in keeping with the interests of their sex."

Raising his eyebrows, Albert Medhurst swallowed another sip of his gin. The conversation shifted to other matters including discussions about business, about the antics of The King and about the weather. Eventually, after an extended period of discourse, Albert said to his friend, "Well, Walter, I should like to continue these conversations on another day.  The hour is very late, and I must be off.  I must sleep and dream my very proper and complex Englishman's dreams, although in this, I think I envy the savage.  I should wish to sleep unencumbered by such vexing complexities."  Lighting a small lantern from the candle on the table, Mr. Medhurst was up from his chair.

The senior bookseller walked his friend and employee down the stairs and outside.  He stood at the roadside until the latter had traversed the few hundred feet to the door of his abode, a scant block away.  Albert lived in a single room over a cobbler shop.  The journey from the bookshop to this nearby sanctuary, while short, was not without its perils.  Robbers may lurk in dark holes or alleys in the night, so Walter always stood guard at the door until he saw Albert step safe inside, always at the ready to render aid and raise the alarm.

Both men, upon returning to their respective abodes, quickly retired.


The following morning brought a light rain and a cool wind.  Mrs. Hewitt prepared breakfast for Mr. Boniface, as she did each day of the week save for Sundays.  In a daily ritual that was somewhat uncommon in that rigidly class-oriented society, the housekeeper then sat down with her employer and shared the meal that she had just cooked.  Walter Boniface did not believe in the concept of one group of people being socially better than another.  Mrs. Hewitt was his employee and as such, she was paid to cook meals and keep house.  However, he refused to follow the societal norm which would have him look upon her as being of a lesser class than he.  The two ate the same food, at the same table.

Mrs. Hewitt was just clearing away the dishes from breakfast when Walter heard the shutters being removed from the shop below.  He hurried downstairs to find Albert Medhurst along with the shop boy, John Kenworthy, completing their task.  "Good morning, Mr. Medhurst.  I imagine you will be off to seek out the book by Erasmus that we discussed last night."

"That I will, Mr. Boniface," replied the junior partner, the familiarity of the previous night's visit in the upstairs parlour being replaced with an air of formality during business hours.

"Good.  Good.  And keep a keen eye out for any other works of note as well, at a less than fair price, of course."  With a knowing nod, Albert Medhurst departed briskly up the street, preparing to canvass the many small shops and to parley with the many contacts that he knew so well.  "And John," continued Mr. Boniface, turning to the boy, "Sweep out this shop.  There is more mud in here than in the street.  Be smart about it!"  The shop was not really as dirty as all that.  The friendly banter between the shop owner and his young employee was another example of the conviviality with which the bookseller treated all people around him.

As John swept the shop, (although perhaps not smartly,) the senior bookseller examined and organized his arrangement of rare and valuable books.  Alongside these treasures could be found many other volumes which were not at all rare and would sell for quite a modest price.  The little shop catered to all readers, regardless of budget.

As the first few hours of the day passed, a small assortment of prospective customers came and went.  Only a single sale was processed – a rather banal tome about seventy years in age explaining with authority every reason that the monarchy in France would certainly endure forever.  Profits from the sale of this superseded treatise would scarcely pay the boy's wages for the morning, but Mr. Boniface was unconcerned.  It was seldom these walk-in customers that earned the bookseller significant amounts of money.  The most discerning buyers rarely visited the shop in person, but instead sent around their card, most often accompanied by a letter outlining their desires.  Messrs. Boniface and Medhurst seldom failed to locate a copy of a book that such a distinguished customer desired.  If it existed in London anywhere outside of the King's Library, it would not be overlooked.  If it did not exist within the metropolis, enquiries would be sent by post to distant places.  Once found, the book was resold to the buyer at a fair, or occasionally, more than fair profit.

Consequently, when a person sauntered in from the street, even if reasonably well dressed and looking quite respectable, Mr. Boniface would usually allow his partner, or the boy, to serve that gentleman or lady. He would spring forth to help the rare customer who presented a truly aristocratic bearing, but there was one class of customer that he watched for most of all.  When a servant entered upon an errand for his master, Walter Boniface rushed to that man's aid.  In the many years that he had been a bookseller, the great majority of successes in both the sale and the acquisition of books had begun with a visit to the shop by the servant of some avid and wealthy collector.

And as chance would have it, very early that afternoon Mr. Boniface noticed one of these most favoured shop visitors lingering in the street, apparently attempting to muster the courage to step through the door. At that very same moment, Mr. Medhurst was arriving in a cab on his return from the morning's errand, (having been successful in his search for the French translation of the Latin book written by the Dutchman, as well as in his search for other fine books at low prices).  He also noted this servant outside the shop and resolved to delay his return to allow the moment to play out.  The nervous man finally entered the bookshop and mere seconds later, young John exited.  The junior partner in the business approached the young employee in the street.  He asked if the servant in the shop was delivering the card and letter of one of the shop owner's most favoured customers.

"It seems so, Sir," replied John.  "The master booted me out right fast when the man entered.  He took great interest in the customer.  I think he might be representing a seller."  Of course, before books could be sold, they must be acquired.  The acquisition of books at the lowest possible price was every bit as important as their sale at the highest possible price.

"Well then, John," replied the laden Mr. Medhurst, "I will go to my room above the cobbler for a biscuit and a cup of tea.  Come and inform me at once when this man leaves the shop."

"Right Sir, I most certainly will do that."


As one of the bookshop's employees kicked stones in the street and the other drank tea in his own abode, Mr. Boniface was discussing matters that would secure the wages of both for some time to come.  He was told the story of a good doctor of The City who had grown old and had suffered a nearly complete failure of his vision.  As such, he could no longer practice his profession.  He was preparing to retire to a small cottage in the countryside and would need to dispose of an extensive personal library.  He had sent this servant with a thick stack of papers detailing the contents of said library.  The doctor required the sum of five-hundred pounds for the entire collection, but payment must be made, and the books removed the very next day.  He had sold his house and was obliged to vacate it at noon on the day thereafter.

Walter Boniface, upon seeing the list of titles on offer, was not entirely successful in suppressing a squeal of excitement.  To the bewildered servant, this expression of excitement fell on deaf ears.  Or, perhaps he simply cared not.  The man was likely aware that there would be no more room for him at the doctor's retirement cottage than there would be for the books, and that he would soon face termination.  What did he care if the old doctor took a low price for his library?

Becoming more composed, Mr. Boniface looked at length over the list of titles, upon which was also noted the binding and condition of each book.  It was an extensive list consisting of some hundreds of distinct titles, many in several volumes.  Drawing upon his many years of experience in the bookselling trade, he judged the most valuable twentieth part of this collection alone to easily be worth the five-hundred-pound price for the entire library.

A short distance up the street, Albert Medhurst, his tea finished, had dozed off.  Waking up and finding it to be mid-afternoon, he became angry at John for failing to keep is promise of informing him when the servant left the shop.  He gathered up the morning's acquisitions and trudged down the stairs from his room above the cobbler to express his displeasure.  To his surprise, he found that young John Kenworthy still stood outdoors, shuffling his feet in the doorway of a closed-up store across the street from the bookshop where he had sought feeble shelter from a brief rain shower.  Mr. Medhurst, scarcely believing that the discussion could last so long, asked, "I say, John, are they still in there?"

"Yes, they are, Sir.  I go across the street to help any other customer that comes.  I sold a book to a tradesman that came in looking for something on carpentry in church altars," he reported, beaming from ear to ear and showing a silver coin as proof of his accomplishment.  "He says I pointed him to exactly what he was looking for."

"Hmm... Well done John.  Here – help me with these heavy books."  Albert Medhurst unburdened himself of most of the stack.  The most valuable book, the one specially wrapped, the one written in Latin by a Dutchman then translated into French and destined for sale in England, this book, he held onto himself.

Some minutes later the servant, at last, departed the shop and the two employees re-entered.  Immediately upon entry, John tried to present Mr. Boniface with the silver coin for the book he had sold, but this was received with a wave of the hand and the single word, "Later."  Next, Albert Medhurst tried presenting the good news about the morning's expedition, but this effort was received with a second wave of the same hand and the words, "Also later."

"Mr. Medhurst," exclaimed the shop owner, "We may have an extremely valuable treasure-trove of books on our hands; one that we can obtain for a song, but we must act fast.  Place your purchases of this morning on the table in the rear – these can wait until tomorrow for sorting and processing.  Now, you and I must ride into The City to see an elderly doctor."  Turning to his younger employee, he said, "John, we will need you to mind the store for the remainder of the day.  You have sold books many times and we trust you with this task.  Should any of my most favoured customers enter, tell them that I am unavailable, and likely will remain unavailable tomorrow.  Take their cards and assure them that they will be contacted forthwith."  John had never minded the store alone before and was somewhat nervous.  Still, he looked forward to the chance to make some sales as he found himself quite short on money at that moment.

A cab was hailed, and the pair of booksellers soon found themselves rumbling over the rough road toward a house in Great Prescot Street.  "I've never seen you so eager to leave the shop," observed Albert Medhurst.  "Are you certain that young John can manage things?"

"I am sure that the boy can manage any circumstance that may arise.  We have been offered an opportunity that is not to be missed.  My dear Albert, today I have sold one book, and young John one more.  After the cost of the books, we have taken about three or four shillings in profits, scarcely enough to cover wages alone, not to mention other expenses.  But this collection may have a value of several thousands of pounds, and what is more, I am offered the lot at just five hundred."

"Still," cautioned Mr. Medhurst, "Five hundred pounds is no small sum.  Are you certain it will come across as a wise investment?"

"We shall fully examine the goods before committing to the bargain, yet if those books listed on the papers shown to me by the servant are indeed to be found in this old physician's library, they are worth the price asked and many times more."

"But you will try to get them for less, will you not?"

"Of course I will, Albert.  You know me well."  Mr. Boniface was accustomed to paying the lowest possible price for merchandise, and not a ha'penny more.  His partner flashed him a knowing smile.

In the privacy of the cab, Albert asked a question that he would not have spoken in the shop, at least not during hours of regular business. "Tonight, Walter, shall we have drinks in your rooms, or in mine."

"I would like to be your guest this evening," replied Walter Boniface. Even though Albert's little room over the cobbler shop was small and rather poorly appointed, it did have one advantage.  Albert did not have a servant.  "Tonight, my dear friend," Walter continued, "we shall tend our own fires."

In an intolerant age, the two gentlemen had adopted the phrase, 'Tend our own fires,' to advise each other, even in public places, that they wanted to spend the evening in a private and intimate setting.  For Walter and Albert shared great personal affection for each other.  The vernacular, albeit derogatory, term for them, in that day, was *'Mollies'*.  They were two men who were sexually attracted to each other, and who expressed that attraction physically.

Should these two ever be discovered in the expression of their love, the outcome would be catastrophic.  The socially stagnant and rigid society, spurred on by the even more rigid and piously intolerant views of the church, held such acts as abhorrent and unnatural.  Being found out would likely be fatal.  An odious law remained on the books; one decreed nearly three centuries earlier in 1533 by Act of Parliament and given royal assent by King Henry VIII.  The law dictated that should anyone be found to have committed an act of *'buggery,'* they…

> *"…Should suffer such Pains of Death, and losses and Penalties of their Goods, Chattels, Debts, Lands, Tenements and Hereditaments, as Felons be accustomed to do, according to the Order of the Common Laws of this Realm; and that no Person offending in any such Offence shall be admitted to his Clergy."*

Only a handful of years earlier, a group of men had been arrested in Vere Street, not too very far from Walter Boniface's book shop, and convicted for contravention of this statute.  Two of them hanged for their supposedly *unnatural crime,* including a 16-year-old boy by the name of Thomas White.  Four others suffered cruel abuse in the pillory.  Indeed, an excess of caution was obligatory.

After a rather long and rough ride, the cab stopped in front of a brick house on Great Prescot Street.  Mr. Boniface paid the driver, adding a reasonable gratuity, and the pair walked up to the door.  The ground floor of the house was configured as a doctor's surgery, but it was locked and closed.  The bookseller rang the bell, and a female servant came to the door.  Both gentlemen presented their cards, and the servant escorted them up the stairs from the ground floor to a large room on the first floor, the very room containing the collection of books that had prompted this visit.

At an antique desk in the centre of the room sat a grand old gentleman with immaculately trimmed white whiskers, wearing a finely tailored black jacket augmented by a cravat tied in the Osbaldeston style.  To help himself rise, he leaned heavily on an ebony cane with a carved ivory hound's head on its top.  By his mannerisms and style, he looked every inch the City doctor.  He reached out a hand in the general direction of the pair of booksellers to make their acquaintance.  In a steady voice, he announced, "I am Thomas Paynter, Physician.  Sadly, I have examined my last patient.  My own eyes have failed me, and I know, better than most, that I shall never recover my vision.  That which surrounds us is all the books I have collected in my lifetime, combined with all the books my father collected in *his* lifetime, and my grandfather before him.  I was once blessed with two sons, but both are lost in the recent war with France.  I was blessed with a wife, but time took her.  I greatly regret that I must vacate this residence in two days hence.  Therefore, I seek five-hundred pounds for this collection of several lifetimes, but the amount must be paid in full, and the books removed before the set of sun tomorrow.  For myself, I shall retire to a small cottage in the countryside, away from the noise and pollution of The City. There, I shall enjoy the songs of birds and the smells of wildflowers, or so I am told at any rate."

Mr. Boniface looked very quickly around the room.  "Is the bargain, Sir, for all of the books in this room?"

"It is," confirmed the old doctor.

"Then, Dr. Paynter, may I say that the bargain is struck."  Mr. Medhurst was slightly taken aback by the fact that his friend, contrary to his nature, did not haggle over the deal.  Nevertheless, even his own experience in the trade of bookselling was sufficient to recognize the immense value of this library.  To deprive a sad old man of twenty or fifty pounds in the face of such potential profit would be a paltry act indeed.

Some minutes were devoted to the particulars of timing and payment, as well as the removal of the books thereafter.  After departing from the house in Great Prescott Street, the booksellers visited their banker to arrange for a secure document to facilitate the transfer of funds.  They also arranged for four carts and drivers to arrive in front of the house not too very early in the morning on the following day, and they hired a pair of constables to provide security for the valuable books on their journey through London's dangerous streets.

It was half an hour past closing time when the two gentlemen returned to the shop in Westminster.  John had put up the shutters, but he remained within the shop, awaiting their return.  He was happy to report slightly over two pounds in sales on the afternoon.  Being entitled to a twentieth part, he would receive two shillings in commission, this being over and above his regular daily wages.  He had used all his skills at salesmanship in the attempt to earn four shillings, as he had a pressing need.  Nevertheless, he did find himself in possession of more than he expected to have.

Mr. Boniface advised John of the successful transaction.  He also discussed with him plans for the following day.  John would travel along with Mr. Boniface to Great Prescott Street and together, they would oversee the loading and transportation of the books.  He advised John of the security arrangements and explained that the two of them would ride back to the shop on the carts along with the books, keeping a close eye upon them for the duration of the journey.  John confirmed his comprehension of the plan, then left for the day.

After a dinner prepared by and shared with Mrs. Hewitt, Walter and Albert repaired to the latter's room above the cobbler shop.  Conversation was not the only thing they shared, yet that conversation was of the highest quality.  Albert began, "Walter, last night you said something that I should have quarreled with you about, but I was tired and had consumed too much gin to raise a well-constructed objection."

The senior partner responded with genuine concern, saying, "May the heavens forbid that I should leave you with an unresolved quarrel.  What is it that I have said?"

Albert explained, "When we spoke of dreams, you asserted that the savage cannot dream with the same complexity as you or I.  I contest that.  While the particular imagery of such a person's dreams may differ, how can we say that they do not experience the same complexity as do we?"

For a few moments, Walter subconsciously sipped his gin while deep in thought.  Eventually, he said, "Before proceeding with that discussion, Albert, I too may have a point of contention.  I find that the word, *'savage,'* does somewhat bother me.  Just as you have mentioned, it was late last night when we had that discussion and I too found that the drink was too well sampled to permit me to raise an effective objection.  I do, of course, know what English or European society intends to convey through the use of that word.  It generally refers to one who is not an adherent to one of the Abrahamic faiths, and whose lifestyle is less altered from primitive times than is our own.  Yet this so-called savage usually lives without the choking coal smoke and the stinking rivers that we are forced to endure every day.  He lives in a complex and rich culture.  His culture does differ from our own, yet it should not be dismissed out of hand.  In some ways, perhaps not in all, but certainly in some, I envy him."  Walter's expression appeared noticeably awkward as he continued, "Additionally, when most English persons use the word 'savage,' they do so with disdain.  Most often, the people thusly described are in possession of skin different in colour from our own, and the word is applied to suggest that such a person might be inferior to the English, or to other European peoples.  I do not believe such a person to be inferior in any way.  He may well experience a lifestyle and culture that are often quite different from ours, as Englishmen, but we must, at all costs, avoid the misconception that something is inferior simply because it is different.  Sadly, that error is made all too often by people of this nation.  I think it best if we banish the word, 'savage' from our vocabulary, lest we be misunderstood by those who would use it less charitably."

Albert in no way disagreed.  The use of the word was so common in the society that surrounded him that he had begun saying it without due consideration.  In his friend's explanation of a well-considered opinion, he saw his error exposed and he immediately resolved to correct it.  He quickly conceded, "Your point is well taken, Walter.  Let us, by way of example, discuss just one group of people that our supposedly 'civilized' English society commonly refers to by the unflattering appellation of 'savage.'  Let's discuss, for example, those men who live in the southern part of Africa in a manner largely unchanged in recorded history."

"That is reasonable," Walter responded.  "And harking back to our discussion of last night, could a man who has spent his whole life in southern Africa and who has never learned how to read a book, to make financial transactions at a bank, or ridden in a horse-drawn cab, dream of concluding a complex bargain such as we did today with agreements for purchase, of securing money transfers, of bills of sale, of contracts for carters, constables and the like?"

"Certainly, the individual who you refer to could not dream of such things if he does not know that such things exist," responded Albert. "But could Londoners, such as ourselves, dream of hunting game for our food, or evading an attack by a lion, these being skills necessary for the very survival of the southern African native?"

Walter replied with certainty, "I dare say that we could dream of such things.  I grant that the man we discuss would be very much superior to us in the accomplishment of these tasks when awake, but it is nonetheless endemic in either you or I to have a broad comprehension of the chase, be we predator or prey.  These skills are part of our nature, even if our mastery of them has atrophied in what we commonly refer to as *'civilized society.'*"

Conceding his defeat on this individual point, Albert asked, "What do you think it is that makes our society believe, right or wrong, that it is civilized to a greater degree than that of the Africans?  Is it our law, or perhaps our religion?"  He looked to his friend for a response.

Walter Boniface thought for a moment before responding cautiously. "The leaders of England's favoured religion may claim that adherence to the Christian faiths makes us more civilized, but I strongly disagree.  The African people have religion as well, but I believe both theirs and ours to be equally unconstructive and irrelevant to the definition of *'civilization'*.  Is our code of law a mark of our civilization?  Perhaps to a degree, yet the Africans have laws as well.  These are very often transmitted from generation to generation by oral teaching instead of being written on parchment by parliament, yet they are laws, nonetheless.  I do not think that there is anything endemic in our legal codes which defines us as being more civilized than the African peoples.  I think the source of our arrogant view that we are civilized stems from the fact that our own society has defined the meaning of the word, *'civilized,'* and unsurprisingly finds itself adhering to that definition."

Albert offered a different hypothetical scenario.  "If an infant boy of the African people somehow found himself being raised by a well-to-do

London family as their own, there to be educated as a respectable English gentleman, would that individual be under any encumbrance as a result of his African birth?"

"I can think of just one encumbrance," replied Mr. Boniface.

"And I can think of the same encumbrance," said Albert, with a look of disgust noticeable enough to be seen by the dim candlelight. "He would be rejected based exclusively upon the hue of his skin. How does that speak about our supposedly enlightened society?"

"Poorly indeed," replied Walter, sincerely.

"Very poorly, I should think." Albert sipped his gin and paused to allow for the processing of this most distasteful truth. He continued, "Nevertheless, if that boy could somehow overcome that encumbrance, would he be as likely to succeed in his life's complex endeavours, and therefore to dream in the same manner as those who come from long lines of English parentage?"

On this matter, Walter Boniface had no doubt. He replied, "Without question, such a child, if that one encumbrance were negated, would have as great a chance of success as a child of English parents. Also, his dreams would not suffer for complexity."

Albert suggested, "Then may we conclude that the man who remains in Southern Africa and never comes to England is as capable of complex dreams as we? The complexities that he experiences differ, to be sure, yet are they any less in quantity?"

"But what of technologies that are unknown to an African man?" asked Walter. "I do not suggest that an African man is incapable of imagining the complexities of English society, but only that he is unfamiliar with them. We have the steam pump, and indeed the iron foundries that produce its parts and the coal mines that produce its fuel. We have multi-storey buildings of brick. We cross wide rivers, such as the Thames, on grand bridges of stone. We have ships that cross the oceans.  The African people do not have these things, at least not unless introduced to them by Europeans.  They therefore cannot dream of them, yet these are the most complex of things, I think in all the world."

Albert refilled both glasses with gin.  Thoughtfully, he suggested, "It is true that the African people do not have these things, but do they need them?  We, the English, have chosen to live in a cold and damp climate while the African lives where it is warm all the year long.  We have heeded our own scriptures that tell us to be fruitful and multiply, while the Africans' numbers have remained broadly the same for countless generations.  We need coal to keep our great numbers warm in winter because we have long since cut down the trees that once provided wood for heating and cooking.  The African carefully manages scant fuel so that it is not exhausted.  We also have the steam pump, which re-moves water from coal mines so that men may toil in the bowels of the Earth.  The coal that does not warm our homes is dedicated to fueling the steam pumps so that the miners may dig for yet more coal.  In dif-ferent mines, men dig for iron so that they may build yet more steam pumps.  The African does not have these things as he does not need them.  Consequently, he does not dream of them.  We cannot dream of things that we know not of, and neither can he.  In that, we are entirely alike."

"But Albert, we do know of the wilds of Africa.  We may know very few details about them, but we do know of their existence.  Our dreams may err.  They may show us incorrect visions of the African landscape, such as elephants climbing trees or ostriches flying.  Nevertheless, we are aware that elephants and ostriches exist, and we may dream some rep-resentation of them, even if inaccurate.  The African man who has never been to a great, modern city cannot dream of the complexities of a great city as he has neither seen one nor has any knowledge of its exist-ence."

Albert countered, "As you have said, you have never been to Africa, yet you know of its existence and therefore can dream of that place, even if inaccurately.  Being told that a city such as London exists, the African man may dream of it in exactly the way that we may dream of the os-triches and elephants of his home continent.  As do we in our dreams of his homeland, he would certainly err in his envisioning of ours.  He may dream that our lands have carriages that propel themselves without horses, or that great metal birds carry men and women across the skies, yet he could still dream of a great city like London."

"Well, Albert, I suppose that an African man would think our dreams to be plain and unmeaningful if he could witness them, and that he would adjudge his own to be complex.  I guess our discussion has come to the conclusion that men all around the world are much more the same than they are different, and that we simply view our surroundings from dif-ferent points of view.  As Englishmen, we naturally think that our views are correct, but a native of Africa, the Americas, Australia, China or any other land would think his views to be equally correct."

Albert smiled at his dear friend.  "I agree, and I think our convoluted dis-cussion has finally come to a consensus."

The hour was growing late, the gin was running low, and discussions of grand ideas were becoming difficult to formulate.  There were other, perhaps more enjoyable matters to pursue this evening, so the conver-sation ended for the night in favour of these endeavours.

Very late and under the watchful eye of his dear friend, Walter Boniface walked the hundred and some yards back to the rooms above his bookshop, and quickly entered the world of sleep.

## Chapter 2 – An Extraordinary Opportunity

In a vivid and complex dream, Walter Boniface was riding in a cab along The Strand.  The pavements were lined with African men clothed in their native attire, or at least as such attire was commonly depicted in books written by the so-called *civilized people* of Europe.  There was also a large steam pump operating where Temple Bar should have been.  Beyond the pump, sailing along Fleet Street, was a Royal Navy ship of the line, on a collision course with both the steam pump and Walter's cab.  Moments later, the dreamer found himself back in his bookshop.  John Kenworthy was stealing a shilling from the cashbox.  "Only a shilling?" Walter asked, confused.  John responded by saying that it was all he ever wanted.  Suddenly, money, both notes and coin, began erupting from the cashbox as John grinned in disdain.  Then the cock crew.

Walter did not know then, nor ever, if the crowing of the cock was a part of his dream or if it happened in the waking world.  Either way, he found himself awake at an hour which was very early indeed.  If any hint of dawn's promise was visible, it was confined to the east, and his window faced west.  It was far too early for Mrs. Hewitt to have breakfast ready, so he rose quietly and lit a candle from a fireplace ember.  He took this to the little writing desk in the corner of his bedroom and there he wrote the details of this dream in a diary that he kept for the purpose.

Walter had just dreamt of African men, but he had never actually met a man who was a resident of that continent.  Of course, there were many Negro men and women in London, yet these people had generally arrived there via unhappy paths, usually related to the shameful and barbaric slave trade.  Their clothing was most often in keeping with English traditions and not that worn in their native or ancestral homes.  These were not the people who had appeared in Walter's dream.  On the contrary, he had dreamt of people who still lived in those distant nations, and his mind had transposed them to the streets of London.

Unfortunately, Walter knew very few facts about the people of Africa. He didn't know how they truly dressed, how they styled their hair, how they painted their bodies, how their culture and society functioned, or indeed, very much else about them at all.  He could draw only upon what he had read in books, some of these being illustrated with crude woodcut images.  These books depicted wild-looking beings, appearing quite different, in a great number of aspects, from Englishmen.  Furthermore, he lived in a society that habitually regarded Africans as inferior beings.  Even to a liberal-minded person like Walter who categorically rejected this odious view, it was impossible to entirely purge the oft heard rhetoric from his mind.  Matter-of-fact comments asserting the superiority of white Christians over all other men were heard as a constant background din, and it was impossible to shut these out entirely. As a product of that society, Walter realized that he had entertained thoughts such as these in his sleep, and he was in no way proud of this fact when he awoke.

Walter spent some time that very early morning at his writing desk thinking about these and other prejudices, and the degree to which he was guilty of harbouring them.  When his mind was functioning fully in a state of wakefulness, he could honestly say that he did not believe that the people of Africa were in any way inferior to Englishmen.  Nevertheless, his views were at odds with those of the great majority of his countrymen.  Some hint of those widespread bigotries had permeated his mind to the degree that in his dreams, when that mind was functioning on a primitive and unfiltered level, it had not categorically rejected these views.  This realization troubled Walter greatly.  He resolved to take great effort to purge such prejudices from all compartments of his mind.

At the normal hour, Mrs. Hewitt arose and prepared breakfast.  As Walter consumed the final bites of the morning repast, he once again heard the shutters on the shop being removed by his two dutiful employees, just as on the previous day.  He hurried downstairs to join them just as the final shutter was being stowed.  "Mr. Medhurst," he said, "please mind the shop for the morning.  Young John and I will travel to Great Prescot Street to oversee the transfer of the doctor's library.  John, hail a cab, would you."

"Hail... a cab... Sir?  How, I mean..."

Walter smiled at his young employee.  "I suppose you have never hailed a cab, have you?"

"No, Sir, and hardly ever ridden in one, save for once or twice with you," John stammered.

"Well, go out to the street and when you see one approaching, wave your arms and it will come to a halt."  The young man went outside.  Turning to his friend, Walter said privately, "Albert, three pounds for the book written in Latin by the Dutchman.  Not a ha'penny less!"  The junior partner nodded to acknowledge his full comprehension of the instruction.  It meant that he should do his very best to get five pounds for the book, but if unsuccessful in that effort, he should accept three.

Stepping out into the street, Walter Boniface found a cab stopped at the side of the road and John darting about, excited by his accomplishment.  The young employee, in his jubilation, started to climb into the cab, then realized that he should let his superior step in first.  He nearly fell into the street in his haste to reverse course.  The shop owner scowled at him with an expression of annoyance, but soon found himself unable to maintain the charade and started laughing.  He got into the cab first, John behind him, and they drove off.

Upon arrival at Great Prescot street, a cart was already in front of the doctor's house, but it was not one of those ordered by the bookseller. This one was being loaded with the doctor's medical equipment, the very tools of his lifelong profession.  Walter watched with some sorrow as these implements of the physician's art were unceremoniously man-handled out through the front door.  Once fully laden, this cart departed and only minutes later, the first of four similar carts hired by the bookseller arrived.

Walter Boniface was escorted by the female servant to the library. There, he found Doctor Paynter sitting at the same desk as on the day before.  With him was a man learned in financial matters who examined the secure bank transfer document, and, finding all to be in order, he accepted it on the doctor's behalf.  Walter Boniface was now the legal owner of the books but as a courtesy, he said, "Doctor Paynter, may we begin to remove the books from your library."

"Treat them well," begged the old doctor.

"Not one of them will be moved except under my personal supervision," Walter assured him.  For some two hours, the final remnants of Doctor Paynter's vision saw faint shadows stripping bare the collection of three generations.  Mr. Boniface took personal charge of the most valuable works while at the same time, watching over John and the cart drivers as the books were moved.  After the last tome was loaded, Mr. Boniface spoke once again to the doctor, thanking him for the amicable transaction.

"What does it look like," asked the doctor.

"I beg your pardon, Sir," responded Mr. Boniface, confused.

"The library without books," explained the doctor.  "I have never seen it like that.  Even when I was a boy, it was full of books.  I have never known this library to be empty."

"I cannot say that it does not look plain in its present state.  It is devoid of the grandeur it possessed just two hours ago."

"I think that I am glad to be blind," replied the doctor.  "I could not bear to see these shelves without books.  I am no longer a healer, and I can no longer read.  What is my purpose now?"

The sorrow that Walter had felt earlier upwelled in him again.  He spontaneously composed some words of encouragement.  "Doctor Paynter, you have long served King and nation.  It is now your time to rest.  You should enjoy the bucolic life in the countryside, the sounds of the birds and the scents of the flowers.  You have paid your life's debt.  Your time is now your own.  Your books shall find new life in the hands of another generation."  The old man sobbed softly as Walter bade him farewell.  They would never meet again.

In addition to the four carters, Walter had hired two constables to provide security for the valuable cargo as it was hauled through the dangerous streets of London.  He positioned John upon the front cart, one of the constables on each of the next two and he himself rode in the rearmost cart where he could see all.  So arranged, they departed from Great Prescott Street on their way back to Westminster.

The journey, at first, proceeded without difficulty, but some minutes after passing St. Paul's Cathedral, trouble found them.

It started with two very young ruffians, certainly no more than eleven years of age, who ran up to the rear of the final cart.  With small knives, they cut through the canvas sheets covering the books and began grabbing at the volumes thereunder.  Mr. Boniface tried to prevent the robbery and, although the boys waved their knives in his direction, he never felt that he was in any serious personal danger.  He raised the alarm but before he could reach the rear of the cart, the young robbers quickly fled, each carrying off a single book.  The two constables disembarked from their respective posts and gave chase.

Almost immediately, the bookseller saw the ruse.  By design, the young boys had led the two constables away from the train of carts, leaving the valuable cargo vulnerable to the actual threat.  Two older boys, each armed with far more threatening knives than their young accomplices, began intimidating the driver of the second cart.  With threats and jabs, they pressed their demand that he step down.  The driver was wounded slightly, then was forced to yield to the knife-wielding boys.  Young John, always alert, immediately disembarked from the front cart and took up the fight.  He scuffled with the first armed boy, eventually bringing that young robber to the ground with a slash from his pocketknife.  John then took after the other older boy who had already cut through the canvas on the second cart and was grabbing at the books thereunder.  This robber, well prepared for the blow, used his own knife to cut John badly.  As John fell, the robber once again made a grab at the books in the second cart, but the four drivers, aided by Mr. Boniface, managed to force him to flee empty handed.

Only two books had been stolen, those by the youngest robbers at the rear, but John lay in the street badly wounded.  "John, my boy, what injuries?"  His employer bent over him with grave concern.

Bravely, John replied, "Oh, Sir, just a scratch."  He tried to rise but immediately realized that it was more than a scratch.  "Sir, I may not be able to work for the rest of the day.  Hope I won't get sacked."

"No fear of that, John.  You will receive help presently."  At length, the two constables returned after having been led on a long and fruitless chase after the two young boys.  They had recovered the stolen books; the boys had dropped them on the ground scarcely a block away from where they had grabbed them.  Unfortunately, before the return of the paid constables, the more serious skirmish had ended with much blood spilled.

Remonstrances for the constables' incompetence in failing to recognize such an obvious ruse would have to wait.  Walter presently reassigned them to care for John.  Handing them cab fare, he left them with orders to convey the injured boy immediately to a doctor who might treat his wounds.  Stepping upon the footboard of the rear cart, the bookseller called out as they rode off, "Constables, promise the doctor any funds that might be required, in my name."  He then ordered the carters to lay the whip upon the horses and they proceeded through the streets at the gallop.  The injured robber was left to the discretion of a member of the city patrol who had lately come upon the scene.

Good fortune prevailed for the rest of the journey and the carts arrived at the bookshop without further molestation.  Despite the episode in the street, the entire library was present and accounted for.  A distraught Walter Boniface advised his partner of the terrible events that had taken place just many minutes earlier.  As quickly as two booksellers and four carters could possibly work, the contents of the carts were unloaded and stacked rather haphazardly within the shop.  Every aisle was blocked with stacks of valuable books such that no customer could have possibly entered.  Consequently, Mr. Medhurst shuttered the shop for the day.  He would remain within as a measure of security while Mr. Boniface quickly hailed a cab and returned to check on John.


After several enquiries, John was found under the care of one Doctor MacPherson, a rather gruff and obstinate fellow who, nonetheless, seemed committed to his profession.  The wounds had been sewn up and the boy's middle part was bound in clean bandages, spotted here and there with fresh red blood.  Some warm rum had been administered, serving as a general-purpose healing tonic.  "He will survive," assured the doctor.  "The knife sliced deep, but I think not through any vital organs.  The cuts must be kept clean and if this is done, they will heal in time.  The two constables assure me that payment for treating the lad would be made forthwith.  I shall prepare the account."

As the doctor stepped aside momentarily, John looked to his employer.  "I'm so sorry Sir to incur this cost.  I will work hard to repay it."

Walter Boniface offered a kind smile, then said, "Your fast and courageous action saved an invaluable collection of books from being pilfered.  Owing to what you did, they are now safely in the bookshop.  I shall see to it that you receive good care until you are ready to come back to work in the shop.  I need you to help me sell those books, at great profit of course."

"Auch, here is the account."  The doctor inserted himself between Walter Boniface and John.  Walter looked briefly at the ledger.  All seemed in accordance with reasonable services rendered.  He paid the amount.  "I thank ye then," said the doctor in the form of a bristly, and rather insincere utterance.  "Should ye ever be needing similar services, Sir, I would be glad to oblige."

To Walter, that offer sounded a bit macabre, but he simply nodded his head to the doctor, then helped John to the cab waiting on the street.

"Not quite as nice a man as old Doctor Paynter, is he Sir," John observed weakly as they drove away.  Walter just smiled.  Before this day, his young employee had likely never met a doctor.  Today, he had met two... and ridden in a cab twice... and been seriously wounded by would-be robbers.  This would indeed be a day that the young man would long remember.

Driving slowly as to not jostle John too much, it was another twenty-five minutes before they returned to the shop.  The sun was beginning to set, but it was not yet quite dark.  John was taken upstairs and placed under the doting care of Mrs. Hewitt.  Mr. Boniface then descended the stairs once again.

By candle and lamplight, Walter and Albert undertook a preliminary sorting of the newly acquired books.  In short, they fell into two categories – there were those which had some value and could be sold to general clientele, and then, there were the rest of them.  This second group consisted of tomes of very great value indeed.  Some were two centuries old, yet most seemed to be in the condition they had been on the day they were printed.   Most were scarcely decayed and only trivially worn through use.  While a few volumes, chiefly those touching upon theories of medicine, did show some noticeable wear, the great majority were pristine.   "Albert," observed a beaming Mr. Boniface, "This is certainly the most lucrative transaction I have ever undertaken.  There are at least four-thousand pounds in these books, all for the investment of five hundred, plus another twenty or thirty pounds in sundries."

"Is it everything you have ever dreamt, Walter?"

This question gave the senior bookseller pause.  In fact, he had often dreamt of lucrative business deals, although not very recently.  Very early that morning, even with the day's transaction pending, he had dreamt, instead, of the people of Africa, or at least what his unconscious imagination thought they might look like.  But that was not all he had dreamt.  His dream had also included an image of young John stealing a shilling from the cashbox, which immediately afterwards gushed forth with cash of all manner.  Might not the vision of John's petty theft represent the payment on his behalf to the prickly Doctor MacPherson?  To be sure, the doctor's bill had cost the bookseller very much more than a shilling, but perhaps even this amount would be as trifling as a shilling when compared to the riches to come.

But surely, this was an unwarranted assumption.  Walter Boniface did not believe that dreams were portents of things to come.  He had on many previous occasions considered the question at length and had always rejected the predictive power of dreams.  The mind in sleep knew nothing more of the future than did the waking mind.  He resolved to reject his previous hypothesis, yet it did seem to fit in with the day's events flawlessly.  Or, perhaps, not entirely flawlessly.  There was no omen of the impending attack by thieves, nor of John's injury.  Forewarning of these events would have been much appreciated by all involved.  Walter was sure now.  Certainly, dreams had no predictive power.  Nothing that he had dreamt earlier on that very day should overturn that view.

"Walter, are you there?"  Albert observed his friend in deep thought, having not answered the question asked of him many seconds earlier.

"Hmmm… Oh, apologies Albert.  I was lost in thought for a moment.  Is it all I have dreamt of?  Not exactly.  I have dreamt of obtaining valuable books, but I think I have never dreamt of a deal with such a large potential profit, either while asleep or while awake.  In that, it is more than I have dreamt of.  I am only sorry that the affair on the way back to the shop tainted the day so terribly."  Changing the subject, he continued, "Tell me, Albert, do you believe that dreams have any predictive power?"

"Certainly not!"  The rapidity and absoluteness of Albert Medhurst's answer took his friend somewhat aback.  "Dreams are echoes of the day," he continued, "which then combine with our thoughts, wants, needs, desires and fears and present themselves to us in the form of jumbled visions.  They know nothing of tomorrow beyond what we can know when awake.  Do you not agree, Walter?"

"I do agree, although on some rare occasions I have questioned that position."  Walter described at length his dream from the night before, including his strange journey along The Strand, which was lined with his interpretation of what African natives might look like in the lands that they and their ancestors had called home for countless generations.  The dream had also presented a steam-pump in place of Temple Bar, and a ship sailing along Fleet Street.  He also recounted the vision of young John Kenworthy stealing a shilling from the cashbox and discussed his proposed interpretation of the imagery.

Albert laughed slightly at the description of the bookseller's dream, especially the part about a British Navy Ship of the Line sailing down Fleet Street.  He then added, more seriously, "The thought that John would steal from the cashbox is as improbable as a naval vessel on the streets of London."

"I know that well, and if last night's dream gave me slight doubt, I feel nothing but guilt for that mote of mistrust.  That boy, at great personal risk, took on a gang of thieves this day and drove them off even as a knife was thrust into him.  He has proven his loyalty once again, even though it was in no real doubt before."

"There should be a reward," opined Albert.

"There will be," assured the bookshop owner.  "Henceforth, he will receive a raise in pay for his cleaning and organization of the shop, and a greater part of the commission for books that he sells.  I will also ensure that he receives more instruction as to our trade so that he may take on a more responsible role in the operation of the shop.  He has already very competently sold many books, and we will certainly be thankful for some help selling the collection we acquired today."

The pair continued to sort and organize books long into the night.  A bit of gin was retrieved from the cabinet upstairs and business and friendship coexisted harmoniously that evening.  The hour had already struck midnight before Albert returned to his room over the cobbler shop.  Walter spent the night on some cushions in the shuttered shop, yielding his bed to his injured employee and also standing guard over the treasure within.  The night would seem interminably long.

## Chapter 3 – A Shocking Revelation

alter Boniface passed the long night with fits and starts. Every noise in the street was imagined to be a thief, a burglar or a murderer intent on slashing his throat for the valuable books within.  During those many hours that he lay awake, there were no invasions of the shop.  Every time he fell asleep, however, he saw the shutters either ripped off or crushed inwards to admit all manner of ruffian.  Time and time again, he awoke with a start, fully prepared to fend off a desperate band of crooks and murderers, only to find that all was quiet.

At long last, the morning dawned with needles of bright sunshine piercing the narrow gaps in the shop shutters.  Walter rose from his makeshift bed.  Mrs. Hewitt was preparing breakfast upstairs.  John was up from bed and sitting at the table when his employer arrived.  He attempted to spring to his feet out of respect, but he was not healed to the point of springing just yet.  As he struggled, Walter motioned for him to remain seated.  "How are you feeling this morning, John?"

With a voice only slightly less chipper than normal, he replied, "I can't say that it's not painful, Sir, but I'm ready to get back to work again!"

"Oh no you are not!" Mrs. Hewitt asserted.  "You need a good many more days of rest."

"Heed the advice of my housekeeper, John.  Your employment will be there for you once you have healed.  I don't want you dripping blood over my expensive books, do I?"  A friendly smile was exchanged between employer and employee.  "Your quick thinking yesterday drove off the thieves and I am most grateful for that."  Mr. Boniface then advised John of his decision to offer him more money for his work.

"Well, I'll need to get well as quick as I can, as I rightly can use that money."  John's employer wondered for a moment exactly what grandiose plans the young lad might have for the extra money, but, of course, that was none of his concern.  He simply gave the boy a kind smile and enjoyed his breakfast.


At the conclusion of breakfast, Mr. Medhurst, uncharacteristically, was not heard downstairs removing the shutters.  Walter undertook this task himself whilst all the time eyeing the cobbler shop up the street for any sign of his friend.  He did observe two unfamiliar men exiting via the door that led to the upper floors of that building, both seeming to cast an eye in the direction of the bookshop as they departed.  Soon after, Albert hurried up the street.  "Confound it, Walter," he said, slightly out of breath, "I've just been visited by a pair from the Bow Street Run-ners."  This term referred to the organization of thief-takers of the day, a group of men charged with capturing crooks and hooligans in the city, a profession similar to that which would one day come to be referred to as 'police.'  "They tell me that the robber subdued by young John yes-terday is dead, succumbed to the wounds he inflicted."

"Oh dear," commented Mr. Boniface.  "But surely, they cannot suspect any wrongdoing.  Those young scoundrels were bent upon robbing us.  John acted quite admirably and suffered a severe wound himself in the effort."

Walter cocked his head slightly to the side as he observed, "They did seem intently interested in young John.  It might be gleaned from their line of questioning that they know something of this matter that they chose not to disclose to me.  I could coerce nothing out of them as to what this might be.  They asked how John came to be in your employ, and although I do know something of the answer to this question, I ad-vised them that they should discuss the matter with you.  At that point, they rather briskly donned their hats and departed."

"Curious."  Mr. Boniface uttered that one word, and not another.  The shop was now open for business and professionalism ruled.  Mr. Medhurst served walk-in customers whilst the senior partner spent

much of the day writing letters to potential buyers of the treasures acquired the previous day.

On that same morning, some miles away in Great Prescot Street, the elderly physician, Thomas Paynter, was taking one final stroll around the
room that until just one day earlier had held the collected libraries of
himself and at least two generations of his forebearers.  He ran his hand
over empty shelves that he could no longer see.  He had, only some
minutes earlier, performed the difficult task of dismissing his male servant of some thirty years.  This was the man who had journeyed to Mr.
Boniface's bookshop two days prior.  The loyal servant was devastated
by the blow, but hardly surprised.  A modest termination stipend in
hand, the man of some advanced years sadly walked off in search of
fresh employment that he would likely never find.  The workhouse
loomed.

The finances of Dr. Paynter were just barely sufficient to retain his female servant.  She entered the library to announce that the new owners
of the doctor's house had arrived.  Despite the early hour, the old gentleman poured one last glass of scotch whiskey from a crystal decanter
at the desk where he had spent much of his adult life, as had his father,
and his grandfather before him.  He greeted the newcomers with as
much grace as he could muster.  Immediately after, the female servant
assisted him to a waiting carriage.  Just before boarding he looked back
at what had been his grandfather's house, which had afterwards become his father's house, and until this very moment, had been his
house.  He saw it now as nothing more than a blurred shadow, scarcely
recognizable through the final remnant of his almost completely failed
vision.  It was a shadow that had been his home for his entire life and
he, also just a shadow of the man he had been, could scarcely bear to
leave it.

He thought of his grandfather, now more than fifty years in the grave,
and he was sure that this old man must be weeping as well.

The doctor reluctantly stepped into the carriage, followed by his sole remaining servant.  The driver closed the door behind them, and they rode off toward a cozy little cottage in a countryside full of bucolic beauty, yet entirely bereft of the only life that the City doctor had ever known.  The five-hundred pounds for which he had sold his library, combined with the sale-price of the house and of his medical equipment would be sufficient to cover his debts, but scarcely more.  He had toiled for a lifetime and had broken even.  He had come out better than some.

The bookshop took in several pounds that day, selling a few of Dr. Paynter's books, and a few items from the general shelves.  Letters were dispatched to many of Mr. Boniface's customary contacts in London and beyond.  Summaries of the most intriguing items in the collection were submitted to noblemen and clergymen, to individual collectors and to well-known contacts at both Oxford and Cambridge Universities.  This collection contained books that Walter Boniface had never seen before and, he would wager, neither had any other bookseller in London or its environs.  He was very hopeful of great profit from his purchase.

Late that afternoon, very near to closing time, the shop received an unwelcomed visit.  The same two constables who had delayed Mr. Medhurst that very morning sauntered ominously through the door. "Good-evening Mr. Medhurst," the first said in a very loud, yet noticeably greasy tone.  He cast his eye toward the shop owner but continued speaking to Albert; "I take this gentleman to be Mr. Walter Boniface."

Walter directly answered the indirect inquiry; "That I am, my good man. In what way might we serve you."

"I am Williams, constable in the service of the magistrate's court.  My subordinate in this service is Johnson."  Williams gave a condescending look at the junior constable, who, as it happened, stood more than half a foot taller than his superior.  "Your boy that was injured in the robbery attempt yesterday, is he well?"  The voice was so loud that John most certainly heard it from the bedroom upstairs.

"He is recovering," Walter Boniface responded cautiously.  "It might be premature to say that he is well."

"Ah, recovering.  Well, we pray that he will recover quickly.  Is he nearby?"  Williams strolled, or almost seemed to slither, about the bookshop as he spoke.

"He is upstairs, in the care of my housekeeper."

"With your housekeeper, I see.  Might we speak with the boy?"

Walter Boniface responded, "At the time of the incident, he was acting in my employ.  I can answer any questions that you might have."

"I somewhat doubt that Sir."  Williams spoke in a tone that caused both booksellers to look at him in anticipation of an explanation, but none was immediately forthcoming.

"Good constable, are you aware of something that I am not?  If so, pray do enlighten me."  Some degree of annoyance could be heard in Mr. Boniface's voice.

"Do you know, sir," oozed the constable loudly, "where young John Kenworthy lives when he is not recovering under the care of your housekeeper?"

Albert had once visited John's home to fetch him outside of normal business hours, so he felt himself the most qualified to answer.  "At a room in Shelton Street, which he shares with several other boys."

"Indeed Mr. Medhurst," Williams said condescendingly, "That is correct. And has he ever provided you with any information about the other boys with whom he shares this room?"

"None at all," answered Walter, quite honestly.  Albert shook his head to confirm that he had no additional information to offer.  Both men were somewhat perplexed as to the relevance of the question.

"Well, indeed, sir," Williams continued to ooze forth, "we paid a visit to that room late yesterday based upon the address written on a letter that we found on the dead boy's person.  We went there at once only to find an older boy therein wearing a jacket splattered with blood.  There were also two younger boys in that sparse dwelling, and they rather closely match the descriptions given by those inept private constables who you had hired.  We felt it likely that these boys were the ones who led those constables on the chase away from their charge.  You see, Mr. Boniface, there were three boys in the room, but five beds.  I pointed to one of the empty beds and asked who slept there.  The youngest boy, a lad of perhaps eleven, blurted out the words, *'That was Charlie's,'* before being silenced by the blood-stained boy.  Following this, none of them would say to whom the remaining bed belonged, but the landlord was quick to offer the information.  He pointed us directly to your John Kenworthy.  He also advised us that the rent for the room was past due."

"This information does indeed raise questions," observed Mr. Boniface.  "Do you mean to tell me that the boy who lay in the street after the robbery attempt was this *Charlie*, of whom you speak?"

"We have no reason to believe otherwise, Sir.  We have taken into custody those three found in the room on suspicion of robbery, and the oldest one also for assault upon your boy.  We are here to listen to his version of this confused tale."

"I will check with my housekeeper to see if he is strong enough to speak to you."

"No, if you please, Mr. Boniface.  We must speak to him before anyone has partaken of the opportunity to warn him of our arrival."  Certainly, the constable's booming voice had already provided ample warning.

"That is not my intention," replied the shop owner, somewhat insulted at the insinuation.

"Perhaps it is not, Sir," the slippery constable conceded, "yet nevertheless, we should like to walk upstairs with you."

Mr. Boniface, forced to admit defeat, said, "Mr. Medhurst, would you please mind the shop."  Turning to the two runners, he invited them to walk up the stairs with him.

As they mounted the stairs, Mrs. Hewitt was given quite a fright.  She had heard the commotion downstairs but had difficulty making out exactly what was being discussed.  Her employer walked softly on the stairs, as a gentleman does, but the two constables thundered up as if a herd of elephants were approaching the first floor flat.  Their noise completely drowned out the more refined footsteps of Mr. Boniface, leading her to believe that the wearers of such heavy boots were unaccompanied by anyone less brash.  When the door opened and the bookshop owner entered, she grasped her heart.  "Oh, good Sir, thank goodness it is you.  I thought to be…"

Her voice trailed off as the two officers entered.  "Mrs. Hewitt," Mr. Boniface explained, "These two men are constables from the Bow Street Runners and they wish to ask young John a couple of questions."  The use of the informal and somewhat derogatory term for the officers of the Magistrate's Court caused Johnson, the subordinate officer, to bristle with some annoyance to the point where he seemed about to speak.  However, even as his mouth started to move, he suddenly closed it again and remained mute.

"I'll fetch him," said Mrs. Hewitt, reluctantly, after looking to her employer for non-verbal confirmation of his desire that she should comply.  She stepped into the bedroom and shortly there after returned with the still weak John.  He was helped into a chair next to the wooden table in the kitchen.

"Are you John Kenworthy," Williams asked loudly.

"That I am, Sir."

"Where do you live, John Kenworthy?"

John gave the address in Shelton Street that was already known to the officer.

"And who do you live with?"

John's face betrayed nothing, but his voice faltered a bit.  "Some other boys."

"By what names are these other boys called?"

John paused for a long second.  "We only share the room, Sir.  We… we don't call each other by name."

"Is that because they don't want you to know their names?"  John didn't immediately answer.  It seems that his answer was inferred from his facial expression since the constable simply fired off another question without waiting for a verbal reply to this one.  "How many boys do you live with, and how long have they been there?"

"Well, Sir," began John hesitatingly, "the number goes up and down. Some come, some go.  Some have been there for a long time, and some are new."

Sitting down on another chair to bring his eyes to the level of John's, the constable asked him pointedly, and in a voice just quiet enough to not be heard in the next borough, "If you ever saw the boys you live with outside of that room, would you recognize them?"

Another long second.  "Well, Sir, if I saw them plain then, yeah, I dare say I would, but if they was running at me or something, then I might not."

"Why would they run at you?" enquired the constable.

"I was just sayin, that if they did, then I mightn't recognize them."

"Do you mean to say that if they ran at you waving knives, trying to steal books from a train of carts in which you were riding, you wouldn't recognize them?"

"I... I don't know, sir."

Williams got up again and slithered around the kitchen.  "Young man, I think that everyone in this room is now aware that those boys with whom you live are the same ones who committed the robbery against Mr. Boniface yesterday afternoon."

"Ah no, that surely cannot be," Mrs. Hewitt interjected.

"Well, everyone *else* in the room is aware," the constable conceded by way of correction.  "One of the thieves is now dead.  He is tentatively identified to be named, '*Charlie*.'  What is certain, by witness statements, is that it was the cut that you inflicted with your pocketknife that killed him.  We now need to understand the full nature of this deed to determine if that act was murder, or defense."

"But Sir, I was just protecting Mr. Boniface's valuable cargo!"

That same Mr. Boniface now felt the need to ask a question of his own.  "John, tell me truthfully.  Were yesterday's robbers the boys that live with you?"

"Aye Sir.  That they were."

Mr. Boniface further asked, "How might those boys have known that a valuable shipment was passing at that day and time?"

His lower lip quivering, John admitted, "We may have discussed it the night before in the room in Shelton Street."

"And John, did you have any knowledge of the robbery before it occurred?"  Walter Boniface's voice sounded at the same time sympathetic and enraged.

Tears welled up in John's eyes and his speech faltered.  "Well, it's like this, Sir.  It wasn't supposed to happen as it did.  The two youngins were supposed to run up to the rear of the carts, as they did, and get the hired constables to chase them, as they did, but they weren't supposed to actually steal any books.  Then I was supposed to take one book, and not a very expensive one, from the cart and hand it to Charlie while everybody was looking the other way, real quiet like.  But instead, Charlie starts threatening the driver, cutting at the canvas and grabbing at a whole bunch of books and when I saw him doing that, I fought him.  That's when he got cut.  I never meant to kill him.  Then James – that's the other boy – he was there trying to steal books too.  He wasn't even supposed to be there.  I fought him too and he stabbed me before the cart drivers chased him off.  Nobody got any books Sir, except maybe the youngins at the back."

"So, in other words," Mr. Boniface continued, more enraged than sympathetic now, "you did plot to steal from me."

"So 'shamed to say I did, Sir.  But I also protected your interests.  We were short on this week's rent at Shelton Street on account of Charlie losing his job, and we were likely to be kicked out on the street.  I thought only to pilfer one book Sir, and not a very valuable one.  I thought you wouldn't even notice.  I'm frightfully sorry, Sir."

Mr. Boniface didn't respond to John, but instead motioned for the two constables to step with him into the stairway.  He said to the talkative one, "Williams, this is a tragic situation.  John does not seem to be the one primarily at fault, although he does bear no small measure of guilt for planning the initial theft.  As the intended victim, I am willing to forgive him any criminal transgressions and deal with him as his employer, if that can be arranged."

Williams' slippery countenance seemed to become suddenly sterner, even as his voice grew somewhat quieter.  "I'm afraid that won't do, won't do at all Mr. Boniface.  He has admitted to taking part in planning a theft, even if not a robbery, with those other boys.  One of those boys ended up dead.  He killed his accomplice in the commission of a crime. Murder between robbers, or thieves, is murder nonetheless."

"But he was defending my property from that very robber," argued the bookseller.

"I concede that there are unusual circumstances, but they are for a court to decide upon, not you or I sir.  The boy must be taken into custody at once."

"But he is severely injured," argued Walter Boniface.  "Being hauled to prison may kill him!"

Ignoring all pleas for mercy, Williams re-entered the kitchen saying, "John Kenworthy, consider yourself in custody.  You will have to come with us."

"But no, that's impossible!" cried Mrs. Hewitt.  "His wounds... Mr. Boniface, stop them... My boy, John..."

Their mutual employer told both John and Mrs. Hewitt in sad tones that there was nothing he could do.  Time was given for Mrs. Hewitt to change some of John's bandages, and for him to put on his proper clothes.  He was then led off.  As he left, Mr. Boniface assured him, "I will ensure that you have good counsel.  And I will not say anything harmful against you."  John, resigned to his fate, gave a smile showing that he was appreciative to his employer (now, surely, his former employer) for his kindness even after this betrayal.


By the time that the constables escorted the boy out to the street, the business day had ended.  Albert Medhurst was just beginning the task of securing the shutters for the night when he saw John being led out under guard.  He was dumbfounded.  His friend came down the stairs a few moments later.  "What?  Walter!  What in all creation?"

At that moment, the bookshop owner could not compose himself well enough to tell Albert the tragic tale. "Later, Albert," was all he said. He helped to close up the shop then the two repaired to the first floor. Uncharacteristically, the dear friends entered the parlour and Walter filled glasses of gin before dinner. Finally, after many minutes and after pouring his second glass, Walter related to his friend the entire sad tale of what had very recently transpired in the kitchen of that first-floor flat. "He did actually plan to steal from me, Albert. My dream came true." Walter brought his friend up to date on all the unfortunate details.

Moments later, Mrs. Hewitt stepped just inside the door to inform the pair that dinner would be slightly behind schedule due to the afternoon's events. Mr. Boniface asked her to enter the parlour and sit with them for a moment. "A sip of gin, Mrs. Hewitt?" She feigned revulsion at the very suggestion then gratefully accepted. "I want to assure both of you that I do intend to do my utmost to help John. That being said, by his own admission in front of the constable, he did conspire to commit theft from me, as his employer. In the attempted completion of this theft, someone ended up dead, by his hand. We need to prepare for the possibility of an unhappy outcome."

Mrs. Hewitt looked horrified. "How unhappy an outcome? Certainly, you do not mean to say..."

"T'is true," observed Mr. Medhurst, "sadly, the gallows cannot be ruled out. I would be most distressed by such a turn of events. Even if John had succeeded at his original plan, the loss to you, Walter, surely could not have been very much."

"I likely would have been entirely unaware of it. I wish he had succeeded and that I had never been the wiser." Walter was sincere in this statement. He truly wished that he had been the unknowing victim of a petty theft as opposed to being an unwilling participant in this sad drama.

Dinner was consumed somewhat later than normal and in sombre moods. Afterwards, Mrs. Hewitt having retired for the evening, Walter and Albert continued to sip gin and speak of the events of the last two days.  "Tragic," commented Albert.  "Four boys locked up in prison, one dead, and for what?  Over the rent-man's want of some shillings, certainly not so much as a pound.  Five lives laid waste over a pittance."

## Chapter 4 – Grand Dreams and Great Men

In the darkness of some predawn hour, Walter Boniface was dreaming. He dreamt that he was in a courtroom. Although nothing was said to this effect, he was aware that this court would soon hear the case of John Kenworthy. A bailiff, or was it a constable... perhaps it was just a turnkey, offered to take him to see the boy in the cells before the trial. He descended the stairs not as one does in the world of the awake, but by gliding over the very tips of each tread. At length, he arrived at a heavily barred cell, inside which sat young John. "Am I to be hanged, Sir?" asked the dreamt John.

At this point, Walter became aware, on some level at least, that he was not in fact speaking to his young employee, but only to a conjured image of him in a dream. By force of will, he passed directly through the stout iron bars and was with the boy inside the cell. In his state of sleep, he presented carefully constructed legal arguments that he thought would exonerate John. Sometimes he was in the cell with the boy and other times speaking in front of a judge trying the case. Walter spoke of John's loyalty, of his sense of duty to his employer, and how this proves that the killing of Charlie was the act of an employee in defense of his employer's property. With every argument, flashes of doubt invaded. There were visions of scowling judges, of the gibbet, of men, women and children cheering at an execution.

As the dream stretched on and the scene returned to John's cell, Walter realized that they were not alone. Another boy was there as well. John introduced him as James, the thief who was not supposed to be present on that unfortunate day. Walter had never seen James, save for a momentary and unclear glimpse during the attempted robbery. He knew nothing of the boy's face, so his dream had conjured that face as pale and blank. Walter turned to this generic figure and said, "I am angrier with you than I am with John. I would sooner see you go to the gallows than he." The pale shade of a boy answered back, "I didn't kill anyone. John shall hang, and not me."

In an instant, the scene shifted once again to the courtroom. Strangely, the cashbox from the bookshop was present on the judge's bench. Bold as day, the dreamt John walked up and removed a shilling. Then, just as before, the cashbox started gushing vast sums of money in all directions. John grinned as he held up the single shilling, ignoring the rest. He turned to face Walter and calmly said, "I have no desire for any more, Sir." With this, the dream ended, and the dreamer awoke.

The fire in the bedroom was cold out; not even an ember from which to light a candle. In the time it would take to strike a light, Walter would forget most of his dream. Fortunately, Mrs. Hewitt was a fine housekeeper. It was apparent that she had arisen in the darkness of night to add fuel to the parlour fire. Once a light was obtained from that source, Walter detailed his latest dream in his log.

After careful review of the questions raised by the unconscious mind some minutes earlier, Walter felt cautiously confident that John could not be deemed guilty of murder. The fatal wounds he had administered to Charlie had been in defense of his master's property and, indeed, he would have been remis if he had taken no action in the face of the attempt at highway robbery. All would surely be well in that regard, he thought. The trial was eagerly anticipated in the ardent hope that it would provide confirmation of that prediction.

The more trivial, yet none the less perplexing part of the dream's imagery was the repeated vision of John stealing from the cashbox. As had been the case two nights earlier, John had wanted only one shilling, and nothing more. He was dreamt of as a very persistent thief, albeit an incongruously petty one. Why did that image repeat itself? Did the shilling represent the book that John had intended to steal from the cart and pass surreptitiously to Charlie? It would have had a value of well over one shilling, yet, once again, Walter considered that perhaps a single shilling represented not a specific quantity of money, but rather an unspecified amount that would be very small when compared to other riches.  He had absolutely no explanation for this aspect of the dream.  This lack of a working theory gnawed at him.

The memory of the dream faded as dawn crept across the sky.  Walter lamented to himself, "Oh, if only the boy *Charlie* hadn't died."  Had there been no death, Walter would have simply allowed this whole sad matter to be forgotten.  Following a stern rebuke, he would have kept John in his employ.  He would have even ensured that the boys could pay their rent.  But with the death, the matter was removed from his hands.  Perhaps rightly so.

In due time, the sun rose fully.  Following sunrise, routine in the rooms above the bookshop remained largely unchanged from day to day.  Walter performed his ablutions as Mrs. Hewitt prepared breakfast.  This day, as he was not detained by slippery constables, Albert Medhurst removed the shop shutters on schedule.  Walter Boniface descended the stairs just in time for the doors to be opened to customers.  There was a comfort in such a stable routine but on this day, John's absence left a gaping hole in the normality of that little bookshop.

Not very long after the shop opened there came a great and very much welcomed deviation from repetitious habit.  The many letters and communications despatched by Mr. Boniface on the day before had already reached some distinguished collectors within the great metropolis.  Word of the acquisition was spreading rapidly amongst the most enthusiastic bibliophiles in London, and among this select group, few were more distinguished than that morning's visitor.

In the minutes following the ten o'clock hour, a carriage of very noble standard, drawn by four magnificent horses, stopped outside of the shop door.  This was accompanied by a detachment of soldiers, some on horseback and some in a second, far less distinguished vehicle.  A footman opened the door to the bedecked carriage, and from that door emerged a gentleman servant.  This individual entered the shop and presented Mr. Boniface with the card of none other than Sir George Spencer-Churchill, 5th Duke of Marlborough.  Four soldiers also entered the shop and took up positions around its perimeter.  Moments later, the nobleman himself regally descended from the carriage.

Walter Boniface was by no means uncultured.  He was in possession of no shortage of manners and dignity, but neither he nor his shop had ever before been graced with a personage of such nobility.  The Duke of Marlborough had once been Secretary of the Treasury under Prime Minister William Pitt, the Younger.  He now sat in the House of Lords.  Few individuals, save for The King Himself, could have made a more splendid customer.  The bookseller was overwhelmed by the magnificence of his visitor.  He bowed deeply.

"You are the proprietor, I presume," said the duke, with a delightfully haughty air.

With a flourish, an introduction was offered; "Walter Boniface, bookseller, at your service My Lord."

"Well then, Mr. Boniface, an Oxford professor currently in residence here in London presented me with a letter, very recently received from yourself, detailing some of the rarest of books that have newly come into your possession.  For myself, I am a collector of rare books, although it is most uncommon that I should travel to a bookshop in person.  Nonetheless, given the rarity and value of some items listed, I felt inclined this morning to undertake the journey with all haste as I should not wish to miss this most uncommon opportunity.  The catalogue of titles found in your letter is truly extraordinary and I dearly hope it to be accurate, lest my ride be in vain.  There are titles included in that list that I did not believe existed in England, outside of The King's Library of course.  I sincerely hope that you shall deliver upon your promise Mr. Boniface."

Mr. Boniface was truly honoured by the duke's high praise of the collection that he had recently obtained.  "The books described are indeed here in my shop, My Lord," he assured the nobleman. "It may interest Your Lordship to hear that they were formerly the property of a venerable physician of The City whose father and grandfather were also avid collectors. They are in truly excellent condition, having been dotingly cared for these many years. Would Your Lordship care to examine the volumes?" The duke, attended by his gentleman servant, accompanied Mr. Boniface into the private office in the rear of the shop, which contained the most unique and expensive works.

As the duke entered the office, Mr. Medhurst was left standing with four officious-looking soldiers. Several more were milling about outside. These attentive security forces barred anyone else from entering the shop, or even from travelling along the street in front for the duration of the nobleman's visit. Moments after the duke entered the office, the captain of this regiment escorted the junior partner in the business out of his own shop and into the street, somewhat to his annoyance. However, Albert's annoyance was mitigated, or indeed eliminated, by the knowledge that one of the most prominent men in the country was negotiating with his dear friend for the purchase of some of the rarest books in existence. He could tolerate the slight humiliation of being expelled from the shop for a short time.

After about fifteen minutes, the duke and the bookseller concluded their discussions. The duke beckoned for two footmen, each of whom carried out a bundle of books. With another deep bow, Mr. Boniface bade farewell to the noble gentleman. The duke boarded his carriage and it, along with the accompanying soldiers disappeared into the bustle of the metropolis.

As the highly distinguished customer departed, Walter met Albert as the latter was re-entering via the front door. The beaming senior partner turned to his friend and said, "I have just concluded a deal for the sale of less than a hundredth-part of the doctor's collection, and for this I received more than was paid for the whole lot." Walter explained that for five individual very rare tomes and a couple of multi-volume series, the duke had paid six-hundred and twenty pounds. On just the second day since Mr. Boniface's purchase of the doctor's library, the large investment had turned a profit.

The next visitor to the shop was very significantly less distinguished. Williams of the Bow Street Runners, along with his silent partner, Johnson, had apparently, for some minutes, been held at bay a short distance up the street by the duke's soldiers. When the duke had finally departed and the officer had managed to slink to the shop door, his annoyance was palpable. In his characteristically very loud voice, he observed, "Well then, Mr. Boniface, friends in high places I see."

"Not a friend, Mr. Williams, but a valued customer. What news, sir?"

"Your boy is currently being held in the cells of the Magistrate's court in Bow Street. On Monday, the fifth day of December, he shall stand trial at the Old Bailey on charges of murder and highway robbery. If you wish to say anything for him, or against him, you shall have the opportunity at that time."

"And of the other boys suspected in the robbery, the ones who John lived with," enquired Mr. Boniface, "when shall they appear?"

"At the same time, Sir. They shall stand together in a common trial."

"And finally, constable, are the cells where the prisoners are currently held open to visitors, and also to counsel?"

"They are to counsel, and as you are an interested party, you may come as well," replied Williams. He added, "In the hours of daylight, if you please. There is no light in the cells after dark." With that, the slippery constable leached away.

On account of Williams' booming voice, Albert had no option but to listen in on this conversation. Once the disagreeable constable had departed, he asked his friend if it was his intent to enter the dismal cells to visit young John.

"Actually no, Albert.  I intend to ask you to go."

"Me, Walter?"  The dread of that dark place washed over the junior partner.

"I'm sorry my friend, but I have sent many letters to those who may wish to view the doctor's books.  I shall need to be in the shop to make presentations.  But rest assured, come the day of the trial, I will speak for John."

"But, the cells… they are so… they frighten me."

"Come now," reassured Walter.  "You are a respectable gentleman, and a valued partner in a business that has just been visited by the Duke of Marlborough.  They will show you the deference that you deserve."


Two short hours after the conversation with his friend, and after securing the services of a competent lawyer to act on John's part, Albert Medhurst found himself in the bowels of the Magistrate's Court in Bow Street.  He was led to see the young man.  Down, he was led along dark corridors, then down some more and finally through steel grates opened by turnkeys and past all manner of wretched men, women and youth awaiting trial.  Finally, his escort pointed to a barred door behind which sat many men and boys, some very young indeed, upon an array of rough wooden benches.  One of these boys was a frightened John Kenworthy.

"Mr. Medhurst, Sir.  I'm very happy to see you, Sir."  John's excitement was obvious.

"How are you holding up, John?  And your wounds; are they continuing to heal?"

"I think Sir that the wounds are doing a bit better than me.  Oh, I've been such a fool.  I see that now.  For hope of a tiny gain, some small income, I've lost everything.  I guess I'll hang for Charlie's death.  I truly didn't want to kill him, Sir."

Albert looked around the cell.  "Are the boys with whom you share your room in this cell as well?"

"No, Sir.  They are keeping us separate.  I heard one of the court officers tell the guard to keep me separate from them.  I suppose they don't want us killing one another before the hangman gets 'round to it."

Albert Medhurst advised John that he had secured legal counsel.  The lawyer would be by to see him presently.  He shouldn't give up hope.  He did, at the end of the affair, act for the benefit of his employer, defending his valuable wares from highway robbery.  The boy killed was indeed one of these robbers.  All these things were in John's favour.  Yet Albert could not help himself from considering the undeniable fact that John was not entirely innocent.  There had been some collaboration with the robbers, conspiracy to commit larceny.  Would a court believe that the young man was not entirely complicit in all aspects of the robbery?  The shadow of the gallows loomed still.  Albert reassured John, "I do believe, John, that Mr. Boniface feels deeply that you should come out of this with, at worst, a light sentence.  He will speak on your behalf at the trial.  If the court permits, he is willing to keep you in his employ.  Don't give up hope."

John bowed his head then looked at Mr. Medhurst once again.  "Will you tell Mr. Boniface, Sir, one more time how very sorry I am for what I tried to do."

"I think he knows, John, but I will remind him."

With little more to say, the two parted ways.  The lawyer visited John later that afternoon, questioning him for every detail of the particulars of that fateful day.  He would be moved to a dismal prison the next day and would see no one familiar until his trial some weeks hence.

By the time that Albert returned to the bookshop, the owner had already put up the shutters.  He sat within the closed shop, awaiting his friend's return.  "Albert," he cried out as the junior partner approached, "What news?"

"John is in spirits as good as can be expected.  Counsel has been retained and there is little more to do until the trial.  He asked me to convey, once again, his regret for what he has done."

"I do know that he regrets his attempt to steal from us, Albert." Mr. Boniface said.  "I just hope that he is given the opportunity to learn from his mistake.  And what of you, my friend.  How are your spirits?"

Albert paused before answering.  "Troubled, Walter," he answered at last, "and confused, but even so, holding their own."  Switching to a lighter note, he asked, "Has the shop been graced by any more dukes?"

"We have welcomed no additional dukes," Walter replied, "but I have served no less than three highly respectable gentlemen who collectively placed another two-hundred and thirty pounds in our coffers for some more of the rarest books.  In addition, several other customers have spent forty and some pounds on more ordinary items.  I have been quite busy in your absence."

"So, tell me Walter, what does that make in total sales from the doctor's library?"

"In all, only two pounds short of one thousand.  All of this for a five-hundred-pound investment made just two days past.  And we have sold less than a tenth part of the collection.  A few sundry expenditures are, I believe, well within our means.  Do you not agree, Albert?"

The primary meaning of Walter's rhetorical question was not lost upon his friend.  While indeed there were sundry expenses to pay for the carters and the inept constables, it was abundantly clear that he was referring to the monies spent for the benefit of young John Kenworthy.  The account settled to the ill-disposed Doctor MacPherson for the treatment of John's injuries was of little concern, not more than a trifle. Less trifling but of scarcely more concern would be the upcoming charges from his counsel.

John was like a son to a man who would never have a son.  In a moment of desperation, or perhaps of insanity, he had thought to betray his surrogate father in the manner of a common thief, and that would forever be to his shame.   Even so, when the threat of highway robbery loomed, his true mettle showed.  He immediately leapt to the defence of his employer's property, fighting bravely against the robbers.  In that act of defense, he had both killed, and had also suffered serious wounds.  An act of such loyalty surely forgave some small and unsuccessful treachery. Walter Boniface willfully resolved to adopt the opinion that in his brave act of defending cartloads of valuable books, John had expunged the fault of his intended crime.  He resolved to aid the boy by any means available to him.

That evening, Walter and Albert sat sipping gin in the flat above the bookshop.  "Albert," began the senior bookseller, "We previously have discussed the question of whether a native of the African continent could dream in the manner that you and I do.  But I propose a question closer to us than the distant continent of Africa.  Could our young employee dream as we dream?  Could John Kenworthy dream with the complexity and depth that you or I dream?"

Taking a long sip, Albert replied, "I do not think that even I can dream in the manner that you do.  I see images in my sleep, but they are disjointed, often frightening and always silly.  You seem to see patterns, experience narratives and develop plots.  Perhaps John cannot dream with that level of complexity, but I dare say that I cannot either.  I doubt that many can."

"But surely, Albert, in your dreams, there are at the very least visions that engender deep thought.  Do you not wonder at the images you see in the night?"

"I do wonder," answered Albert Medhurst, "but I rarely see any pattern or message in the dream.  I have never heard others speak of the complexity of dreams quite in the same manner as you.  Please do not misunderstand me, my very dear friend.  The tales you tell of your dreams are fascinating to hear, but in them I do not find much relevance to our daily lives.  To my way of thinking, dreams offer only a deceitful interpretation of the events that we experience whilst awake.  They pollute the sober, logical proceedings of the day with falsehoods and incorrect assumptions."

Walter found himself rather taken aback by this statement.  It almost put him off his gin… but not quite.  He poured another glass.  "Dreams, my friend, are a reflection, albeit in a glass, darkly, of the day's events.  It is true that these are coloured by all manner of fears, desires and ambitions and echoed by a mind in a state of confusion.  Consequently, they are incongruous and bizarre, but they are in every way honest.  In that state of sleep, our minds are incapable of practicing the art of deception."

"Indeed," huffed Albert.  "If you feel so.  Nevertheless, the honesty of dreams is of little account.  I never remember them."

"Dreams do indeed seem to fade into the very darkness that is banished by the sun.  For my own part, I keep a dream log; a simple ledger along with a pen and ink situated close by my bed.  In this, I record the details of my dreams immediately upon waking whilst they are still fresh in my mind.  Daylight often causes us to unburden ourselves of our nightly visions, yet that burden, if freely borne, opens a window into our very soul.  By promptly recording dreams in a simple ledger, their imagery and nuance may be retained and thereafter focused to our individual benefit.  Why not try this yourself, my dear friend."

"I suppose I could try," Albert admitted with minimal enthusiasm prior to giving the suggestion greater thought.  After considering the recommendation, he decided that he might enjoy engaging with his partner in the pursuit of dreams.  After a few moments, he continued, "Indeed, I will keep a log of my dreams, if only to come closer to experiencing these visions in the way that you find so fascinating."  Having said this, Albert shivered noticeably.  "Oh, the night is growing cold.  Shall I add a log or two to the fire, or should I head home?"

"Do stay, for a short while at least."  Walter moved closer and gently touched his friend on the cheek.  "Add a log.  I am not ready to be alone just yet.  Other fires burn that we must not tend ourselves, not here at least."

"Indeed, never here Walter.  We cannot risk being found out."  Albert gently pushed his very dear friend's hand aside.  There was a short pause.  "Tomorrow evening, will you visit my room?"  That arranged, there was a bit more gin and a bit more conversation.  Eventually, when even this most recent log had been reduced to ashes and embers, Walter watched his friend traverse the hundred and fifty or so yards to the entrance to his own small abode.  Thence to the theatre of sleep.

## Chapter 5 – Business as Usual

Before dawn on that Saturday morning, the heavy dark-gray clouds had opened up and let loose a hard, drenching rain. In the street, depressions in the cobbles carved out by decades of wagon, cart and carriage traffic, flowed with muddy rivulets. Above the bookshop as the rain pelted the roof, the familiar routine played out once again. Mrs. Hewitt prepared breakfast, then shared it with her employer. Afterwards, Walter descended the stairs in time to meet his friend as he removed the final shutters from the shop windows. To some, the routine might have seemed wearisome in its repetition, yet that same repetition helped give structure to the lives of those involved. The shop owner could be counted upon to arrive within that small timespan between the moment when the last shutter was unlatched, and when it was stowed. It was only on a very rare day when he arrived either before or after the completion of this symbolic task. Either was a portent of a troubling day to come. Today, as on most days, he was right on time.

"Good morning, Mr. Medhurst," he called out, following the formality of business hours.

"A very good morning, Mr. Boniface, albeit a very wet one." Albert grabbed a broom to sweep out the previous day's tracked-in mud. Normally, young John would undertake this task, but in his absence, the junior partner stepped into the role. As he swept, he advised his friend, "I heeded your advice. I started my dream log early this morning. I actually wrote a very detailed account."

"I look forward to hearing that account this evening." With that, the first customer of the day came to the shop door.

An elderly man leaned heavily upon a cane as he entered, dripping wet from the still torrential rain. Served by Mr. Boniface, he asked, "Might you, my good sir, have copies of the works of Homer: The Odyssey and The Iliad.  You see, my grandson is reading ancient literature, and I should like to present him with these magnificent works as a gift to mark his twelfth birthday."

"I do have an excellent copy of each work, as translated by the late William Cowper.  The volumes are nearly thirty years in age, yet they have for all that time been in the possession of a physician from The City who has kept them in truly excellent condition."

"I shall look at them," replied the old gentleman.  The books were brought to him.  "The binding is old indeed," he observed, "in the finest leather I think, but they do not appear to be very well read.  They are of some quality.  I expect that you will require a hefty price for them."

Recognizing the gentleman's eye for high quality bookbindings, Mr. Boniface replied, "Of course, my good Sir, there is considerable expense involved in obtaining such fine books.  One must recover expenses, and I require only a small amount for myself."

"Yes, yes," replied the old gentleman, sounding mildly annoyed.  "I shall offer you five pounds for the pair, and not a farthing more."

Walter Boniface responded, "My dear Sir, I would most graciously accept ten pounds for these two fine books, or for a fine gentleman such as yourself procuring a gift for your grandson, I would allow you to take them off of my hands for eight."

"Oh, you would bankrupt an old man.  Six!  No more than six pounds."

"Very well, Sir, as your grandson may be a future customer, I am reluctantly willing to part with them for six pounds."  The deal being struck at a price that appeared somewhat in the old gentleman's favour, he gladly handed over that notable sum of money as Walter wrapped up the books.  Both booksellers bowed deeply to the gentleman, wishing him a very good day as he left the store.

Once the elderly customer had departed, Mr. Medhurst asked the senior partner, "Mr. Boniface, How much were those books actually worth?"

Walter Boniface smiled.  "They were certainly the least part of the doctor's library.  Before the gentleman suggested a price, I had thought to offer them at three pounds for the pair and would have sold them for two."  There was a muffled laugh – laughter was not entirely in keeping with the code of formality adhered to during business hours but as there was no one there to bear witness, the rules were bent slightly.  The bookseller continued, "A silver tongue is indispensable in our trade.  A book is as valuable as we can convince a customer to think it is."

"Unless we are buying, of course," retorted Mr. Medhurst.

"Well, obviously unless we are buying.  In that case, a book is as worthless as we can make the seller believe it to be.  That is our margin, my friend.  Our profits are defined as the inequality between the price for which we can wrest books from sellers and the price for which we can peddle them to buyers, less all expenses, of course."

As the day wore on, a steady stream of customers entered the shop.  The two booksellers attempted to convince them of the value of assorted volumes.  In some cases, they succeeded.  Many customers left with wrapped-up books, a few left without.  Nothing of very great price was sold in the remainder of that day, but many general works left the shop in exchange for a few shillings here, a pound there, and the like.  This was the ordinary manner of business.  It covered expenses and paid wages, and while not as profitable as those rare sales of exceptional books, it was very much welcomed by the shop owner.

Books continued to be carried out of the shop at the highest price possible until, as the sun dipped low in the west, the two men worked together to secure the shop shutters.  After a delicious meal prepared by Mrs. Hewitt, the pair walked a short distance along the street and climbed the stairs to the room above the cobbler.  The gin being poured, Walter was the first to speak.  "Alright, Albert, you dropped a hint early this morning.  You have made your first dream log; let's hear it then."

"Well then Walter, here is what I wrote by this morning's earliest light." Albert read from his log, "I was seated in a cab and was being driven across London Bridge when, quite suddenly, I was not in the cab any longer but instead in a boat beneath the bridge.  The small boat, initially sailing upon the Thames, instantly transformed into a ship at sea.  Shortly thereafter, it landed at some African port, or perhaps I should say African village as it seemed to be entirely landlocked.  The natives I saw there were all dressed in respectable English attire, and even though they were of a darker complexion than most Londoners, they looked in all other aspects like the most proper and upstanding ladies and gentlemen of this city.  One man spoke to me.  I did not understand him at first, and I felt deeply ashamed by my lack of understanding.  He repeated himself, and this time I heard his words in perfect King's English.  Sadly, I cannot recall what he said.  Soon after, I was instantaneously transferred back to London and found myself in Paternoster Row.  I observed the many booksellers in that street, our competitors in the trade.  They asked questions about our recent purchase of Doctor Paynter's library, yet I do not recall the exact nature of these questions. I became frightened by all the attention and ran past St. Paul's, then onto Cannon Street and eventually Great Tower Street to the Tower of London.  In the dream, the distance was much shorter than it is in actuality, and it took only seconds to make the journey.  But each time I arrived at the Tower, I instantly found myself back at Paternoster Row. After this had repeated three, or possibly more times, I saw you in the street, Walter.  You appeared not as my employer but as my friend.  We greeted one another warmly."  Albert then looked at Walter, indicating that his narrative was over.

Walter raised his brow.  "That was a merry dream, of great complexity to be sure, but rather disjointed.  It seemed to be of many parts, these being unrelated to one another."  The experienced dreamer proceeded upon a hunch, "Did it end right where your log left off?"

Albert looked perplexed.  "Confound me, I'm sure that it did not, but I'll be damned if I can recall how it continued.  I think I may have dreamt something of our relationship.  I mean, that part of it which can never be disclosed.  I vaguely recall that I thought it wiser to leave this out of my dream log."

Walter, the more experienced dreamer even if sometimes the less cautious, agreed.  "You are quite correct, Walter.  That subject is something that we must leave out of even our logs.  If any proof of our forbidden love should ever be found out, our lives may be forfeit."

"Indeed, and I am sure that I ended my recording of the dream where I did for that very reason.  Strange, however, that I recall ending my transcription due to the dream's subject matter yet cannot recall the details as to what that subject matter consisted of."

Walter took a sip of gin and laughed a bit.  "I hope it was of us in passionate embrace."

"I hope it was," replied Albert, "and I do think it was something of that nature, but if that were the case, it seems difficult to believe that I would have forgotten the dream.  Why, Walter, must we hurry upon awakening to record our dreams on paper before their memory inevitably fades?  Does it not seem odd that I can better recall what I ate for breakfast than I can a meaningful and exciting dream?"

Walter replied, "Believe me when I say, Albert, that I have been perplexed by that phenomenon on countless occasions.  My personal theory on the matter is that our minds have developed this forgetfulness of dreams, this amnesia if you will, as safeguard against the confusion that would ensue if we mistook the disorderly narrations of our dreams for reality."

"That would make sense," mused Albert, "If I vividly remembered my dream, including the part where I had visited Africa, I might come to accept it as fact that I had indeed made the journey."

"Absolutely," Walter agreed, "And you might regale friends and colleagues with tales of your adventures on that continent that, in fact, had only been dreamt about.  Your credibility would suffer terribly – a trip to Bethlem might be thought in order.  Much better that you forget, is it not?"

Agreement was signified by another sip of gin.  "But as to the imagery of the dream itself, what do you make of it?  Why have we both been dreaming of the men of Africa as of late."

"I think," Walter suggested, "that the African theme arose from our innocent conversation of a few nights ago when we spoke of the dreams of people native to that continent.  Neither you nor I have any idea of the nature and culture of the men who live in the forests and scrublands of Africa, so we invent these things in our dreams.  The images tell us nothing substantive of the Africans, but only of our preconceptions, and indeed prejudices, in their regard.  You dreamt of African men in the clothing that would be common in London.  You do not know what these men actually wear, so your mind dressed them in a familiar style.  As for myself, I dreamt recently of such people in London dressed as I imagined they would dress in their home nations, although I do concede that my impression of how they dress is based on highly biased sources.  Truly, I have no reliable knowledge of how they dress either."

"Perhaps you are correct, Walter.  Although many Negroes live here in London, we can learn from them very little of their native, or ancestral homes."

"Yes, sadly that is true," Walter agreed.  "For the most part, even they do not know of a life in Africa, or if they do, it is only a distant memory.  The majority have come here through the slave trade, by one means or another.  Despite the illegality of slavery in England, I am sad to say that the abominable practice is still rampant in other parts of the Empire, and beyond.  Many of London's Negroes are in fact slaves in all but name.  I have, however, heard tell of one man who, some fifty or more years ago, overcame the enormous burdens that our society place upon those of a darker complexion.  He was a grocer who held a shop not so very far from here.  He was known by the name of Ignatius Sancho and as well as being a shopkeeper, he was a respected letter writer, a composer of music and an outspoken abolitionist.  I recall once coming upon a book of his collected letters.  Sadly, I was not successful in obtaining it for the shop."

"Fascinating, Walter.  I was unaware of Ignatius Sancho."  Albert Medhurst took another sip of gin.  "To pull himself up through the mire of English prejudices and attain such a respected status, he must have been an extraordinary man."

"He does stand as absolute proof that there is nothing in the nature of a man with African ancestry, or of a man native to any distant land, which prevents him from attaining any station in life whatsoever, save, of course, for the bigotries that he encounters along the way."

"You shall find in me no argument of that point, but even so, the tale of Mr. Sancho still does not enlighten me in regard to the lives of men still living in Africa.  If there is any reputable book in the shop on this subject, I should like to buy it.  I do suppose you will try to make the maximum possible profit off me, will you not?"

Walter smiled at his friend.  "I would not be a fine businessman if I didn't, yet to find a reputable source of such information, I think you would need to learn those peoples' native languages and travel to Africa to meet them.  I think it doubtful that any Englishman, or any European, would do justice to the subject."

The fire had died down and needed tending, as did their own fires.  It would be very late indeed before Walter took the short walk along the street to his home over the shop.

Tomorrow would be Sunday.  Walter intended to sleep late, although Albert had definite plans for the early morning hours.

## Chapter 6 – Views to Justice

Sunday morning dawned and Walter Boniface was still dreaming. Even as the sun rose higher, he was still occupying that very different world. Soon after, however, every church in Westminster and beyond began ringing its bells, rapidly divorcing him from that world of imagination and wonder and forcefully catapulting him into the waking state. To a cacophony of bells, he spent some long minutes writing in his dream log before closing it to await later scrutiny.

Sunday, at the living quarters above Walter Boniface's shop, unfolded very differently than the other days of the week. Mrs. Hewitt did not prepare her employer's breakfast on this day. She, being very active in the local church, departed early in the morning to assist in the preparations for services. Walter understood nothing of religious ritual. A faith that would enthusiastically encourage death for him and his dearest companion if ever their nature was revealed interested him not at all. His indifference toward religion was not kept secretive. He was as openly secular as his housekeeper was religious, but this disparity troubled them little. Neither their professional relationship nor their friendship was strained by this disagreement. Each sincerely respected the other for their more material qualities.

Mrs. Hewitt was a kind and generous woman. Childless and widowed at the tender age of twenty-three by the war with Napoleon, she dedicated herself six days per week to Mr. Boniface's service. By their agreement, her seventh day was passed in service to the church. In return for her six days of labour, she received a modest recompense, ate the same food as her employer and lived in a safe, warm home. Walter had even taught her how to read, a skill that she had previously lacked. He felt genuine compassion for the woman who tragedy had made old before her time.

On this Sunday, as on most, Walter prepared his own breakfast and consumed it at the wooden table in the kitchen.  Upon that table sat the previous week's copy of the *British Monitor*.  Mrs. Hewitt would often obtain a battered copy of this tabloid from one or another shop for a farthing or two, several days after its publication.  This offering had previously been known as the *Anti-Gallican Monitor*.  Given the circumstances of the loss of her young husband, one can understand why she chose this title.  On occasional Sundays, Walter availed himself of the third-hand rag when its contents were a full week in age.  Its tone was very often more opinionated than was his taste, but far less so than religious sermon.  It was a bit of entertainment that he enjoyed whilst countless others were sitting in the city's many churches.

Albert Medhurst, while not overtly religious, did attend Sunday services, although not those provided by the Church of England.  Following his family's tradition, he attended mass at a small Roman Catholic church that stood nearby.  He honestly felt that the mercy of Jesus Christ might invalidate the vitriol of his church, which, in a rare moment of full agreement with the Church of England, also sought to eradicate people of his nature.  Walter disagreed with the idea of a merciful saviour but chose not to argue with his friend on this issue.  Neither man claimed any particular expertise in the theory of religion, and they chose to avoid any protracted discussion relating to the subject.

Following mass, Albert generally joined his friend at the bookshop.  There were Sundays when the pair would toil in the shop, often sorting books, agreeing upon prices and performing general maintenance duties.  This was not one of those Sundays.  The November day had dawned uncharacteristically sunny and glorious from the start.  The temperature was unseasonably warm and by the time Albert arrived, Walter was more than ready to leave the roof and walls behind.

The wind being from the south, the two gentlemen headed north in an attempt to place some distance between themselves and the stench of the Thames.  Continuing north from Oxford Circus, they eventually arrived at Regent's Park.  This was a quiet place amidst the confusion of modern, 19th century London.  On this, likely the final warm day before winter, Londoners of all descriptions strolled through its pathways and amongst its trees.  Men and women occasionally expressed slightly risqué affections that were positively forbidden to lovers of other persuasions.  Even so, Walter and Albert cherished their occasional Sunday walks in this peaceful place.

"Oh Albert," observed Walter, "See how the squirrels and rabbits run here and there.  One envies them.  Not a care in the world."

"I see them," Albert responded.  "They are as quick, and almost as numerous as the pickpockets."  With this merry observation, the two sat down upon a bench and Albert asked an unrelated question.  "Two weeks from tomorrow will be John's trial.  What do you intend to say?"

"The truth, and all of it," Walter assured his friend.  "I still hold the boy dear, upset as I am at the betrayal.  I truly believe that in the end of the matter, he acted on my behalf in repelling the robbers.  He certainly erred, but I feel that he has recompensed that error, to me at least.  If the law feels that he must pay a further penalty, then I cannot prevent this."

Albert thought for a moment.  "Surely, he will not be hanged, will he?"

Walter responded, "He conspired in a criminal plot that ended in highway robbery, albeit the most banal performance of that crime that has ever existed.  He, by his hand, killed one of his co-conspirators.  Albert, I do assure you that I shall do everything in my power to prevent that outcome, but we must prepare ourselves for the worst."

"And if the court does exonerate him of capital crimes, will you still employ him?"

The bookseller answered resolutely, "I am resolved to give John Kenworthy the opportunity to redeem himself.  He is ours, my friend.  He is a poor orphan who on one occasion made an error.  Regardless of whether or not he deserves a second chance, it is incumbent upon us to give it to him.  We are the only family he knows.  I, for one, will not turn him out, so in answer to your question, yes, if the court allows, he will still be employed at the bookshop."

After a few minutes of sitting in silence watching a small rabbit chewing at some weeds, Albert suddenly sprung to his feet, waving his arms and shouting with great excitement.  Walter looked up to see what the cause of the commotion might be.  He observed a fox very rapidly approaching.  The kind-hearted Albert was either trying to warn away the rabbit or to forestall the fox.  It was unclear which of these outcomes was his intent, but neither was to any avail.  The carnivore sunk its teeth into the hapless rabbit's neck.  With a macabre chuckle, Walter softly uttered the words, "Circle of life, my friend."

The pair slowly strolled back from the park.  They each advised the other that they had dreams to discuss, but that this would have to wait until they returned to Walter's rooms.  Neither remembered the substance of what they had dreamt, only that their dreams contained bizarre and impossible imagery.

In a strange irony, just as they were discussing the eccentric nature of dreams, the pair caught a distant sight of Chunee, an enormous Indian Elephant, who was being led by his keepers on his weekly walk along The Strand.  Albert commented sarcastically, "Well, it's nice to be in the waking state, where there is never any bizarre or strange imagery."

Elephants notwithstanding, the streets of London were as busy, noisy and dirty on a Sunday as on any other day of the week.  Shopfronts, shuttered for the sabbath, seemed more menacing than when they were open for business.  Churches, unshuttered for the same occasion, presented a similar air.  On a Sunday afternoon, masses of people dressed in their finest attire shuffled about the streets with no particular place to go.  In their lack of immediate purpose, they seemed to cast judgemental eyes in every direction.  Gossip abounded.  Both Walter and Albert felt uneasy.  It was as if ladies in long Sunday dresses might see the friends' deepest secret by nothing more than a glance, or as if the labourers, merchants and tradesmen who, six days per week, sold clothes, cut hair or laid bricks, might have suddenly become spies for The King.  Despite the pleasure of having a bit of time to get away from their place of business, both men felt more at ease when they re-entered the rooms above the shop.

Mrs. Hewitt returned from her religious observances only minutes after Walter and Albert had entered the rooms.  She was not Walter's employee on a Sunday; such was their agreement.  On this day of the week, Walter and Albert prepared a meal (although, by her nature, Mrs. Hewitt could not sit by without offering some help.)  In times past, Walter could not pay this fine woman much in the way of money, so he made up for this lack of financial recompense in kindness.  She wanted for nothing.

As she did on every day, Mrs. Hewitt sat at the table and shared the meal with her employer and his friend.  "I prayed for John today," she said.  "I prayed that The Lord would forgive his transgressions and that he would be freed, or at the worst, given a very light sentence."

"That was kind of you, Mrs. Hewitt."  Walter was sincere in this statement.  He did not believe in the power of prayer, but it was nonetheless a kind act on the part of his housekeeper, who did.

"Oh, you will speak on his behalf when he comes to trial, won't you Mr. Boniface."  Mrs. Hewitt had no tears in her eyes, but they were clearly in reserve just below the surface.

"I assure you that I will do my utmost to ensure that he is exonerated of the serious charges.  He may stand convicted of a minor one, but that should not carry a very severe sentence.  We need him back in the shop.  Mr. Medhurst is weary of having to sweep it out each morning."

Following dinner, the trio collectively cleaned up.  Mrs. Hewitt then excused herself and retired to her room.  Walter and Albert went into the parlour.  Walter spoke first.  "Your dreams last night, Albert, did they focus on John."  His friend answered in the affirmative.  "Mine did, too."

Looking serious, Albert said, "I truly don't believe in any predictive power in dreams.  I've told you that before.  Still, I saw, last night, someone hanging from the gallows."

"Was it John?"

"I don't know," replied Albert.  "I didn't know in the dream.  I tried to find out, but I couldn't get close enough.  There were crowds of people pushing me back."  Albert opened his little dream log for more details, then continued, "Ah, yes, before witnessing the hanging, I was arguing with someone, a man who I did not recognize.  We were out in a street somewhere, but then, all of a sudden, we were in my room, still arguing. I then walked, or rather, floated down the stairs and out into the street. It was this street, but not quite right.  Several of the shops were simply missing and the cobbler that I live above was nearly opposite the bookshop.  I walked down toward Westminster Abbey, then into the Old Palace Yard at Parliament.  This is where the gallows were erected and that's where I saw someone hanging, between the rear of The Abbey and Parliament."

"Not the usual place for hangings," observed Walter.  Seeing that his friend was genuinely concerned, he continued, "John did not commit highway robbery.  John killed only in defence of his employer's property, and the boy he killed was indeed committing highway robbery.  He is not guilty of any capital crime, and I will ensure that the court is aware of this."

"I know that you will do all you can, Walter.  Why do you suppose that my dream placed the gallows in the street between Westminster Abbey and Parliament?"

Walter came up with a theory rather quickly.  "Perhaps the gallows in your dream were not for John, but for us.  Both the church and the state would like to see us dead.  Where else do the grandest elements of religion and governance come so close to one another as in Old Palace Yard?"

"Well, there's a merry thought," commented Albert, sarcastically. "Shall we find some less sombre themes in your dream?"

"As for my dream, I walked into The City and finally across London Bridge, pausing to look east to the Pool of London where there were many ships loading or unloading. On the far side of the bridge was not Southwark Cathedral or the Borough Market as I expected, but rather a seacoast with waves crashing ashore. I then saw a lone ship some distance offshore, and I was instantaneously transported onto that ship. In the hold of the ship was a great treasure of gold and jewels, and, you might guess this part, our cashbox from the shop."

"Again?" commented Albert amazed at the consistency.

"Again, my friend. John stole a single shilling before it gushed forth even more riches."

Albert sipped his gin. "There is an uncanny repetition of that image in your dreams."

Walter agreed, but also questioned his friend, "Why do you suppose that I dreamt that there was an ocean immediately on the south side of the Thames?"

"How often do you actually go across the river, especially by way of London Bridge?"

"Not often, Albert, but I have on a few occasions crossed that bridge. I do know that there is no seacoast at its southern end, yet that is what I insert into my dreams."

Albert laughed a bit. "And I know that gallows are rarely, if ever, erected in Old Palace Yard, yet that is where my dream has placed them. We are both logical, thinking men when awake. Why are we quite insane in our sleep?"

Walter thought for a moment, then offered, "Perhaps it is not insanity, but simply a matter of the mind taking shortcuts.  To be sure, there is no ocean at the south end of London Bridge, but alongside it is the Pool of London where many ocean-going ships load and unload.  Perhaps my mind, being aware that these ships are most often found upon an ocean, simply turned the Thames into an ocean in order to justify the ships of which I dreamt."

"And of my dream of gallows in Old Palace Yard," Albert suggested.  "It is the state, as represented by Parliament, that sentences people to be hanged.  They do this in the name of The King and with the blessing of the English church, both represented by Westminster Abbey.  Just as your mind created an ocean to explain the ships, perhaps mine created gallows to explain my thoughts regarding executions, and place those gallows at the place where the state and the church most closely inter-sect."

Walter considered for a few moments.  Finally, he said, "I view our ex-planations as reasonable, although not necessarily correct.  I've always tried to find literal meaning in the imagery of dreams, while at the same time acknowledging the symbolic and metaphorical nature of what is seen.  I find it hard to accept the conclusion that they are nothing but complete nonsense, although I do admit that sometimes we are incapa-ble of understanding the convoluted mental processes that lead to the images we see at night.  Perhaps our interpretations are indeed wrong, but I do not think that this suggests that the dreams defy interpreta-tion."  Walter observed Albert looking at his empty glass and added, "Might I interpret that you are dreaming of more gin?"

"Actually, my friend," Albert responded, "you got that interpretation wrong.  I've consumed enough for tonight, and it is time for me to go home.  We must both be in a fit state to tend the bookshop tomorrow.  Your letters describing the doctor's books have now reached their wid-est audience.  Suppose another duke, or some other peer of the realm, should stop by.  We do not want to be half asleep."

Walter saw his friend already getting to his feet.  He escorted him to the
door.  The night was foggy, but he was just barely able to see the faint-
est shadow of Albert stepping into the door that would lead safely to
the room over the cobbler shop.  Walter himself then quickly retired.

## Chapter 7 – Halls of Justice

In the span of the next two weeks, both Walter Boniface and Albert Medhurst toiled for long hours in the shop, and the prime of Doctor Paynter's collection was sold.  There were visits from professors, collectors, rival booksellers and other distinguished citizens and the profits had been great.

Also, before the end of that fortnight, winter's grasp had finally fallen upon London and there would be no more pleasant walks in the park before spring.  Eventually, it came to be the night before John's trial.

Even for a dreamer who dreams with purpose and vigour, there are some nights when the complexity and nuance of dreams is commandeered by burdens of the moment.  Walter Boniface's dreams that night consisted of nothing but a staccato barrage of images relating to the trial.  There were angry witnesses, images of violence that had never actually taken place, and foggy, distant views of the gallows.  He wrote no log of his dreams that night, having deemed them worthy of being forgotten.

Mrs. Hewitt produced a breakfast at the usual time.  She and Mr. Boniface ate together, as they did six days per week.  Although her daily routine was unaltered, the housekeeper's face looked uncommonly careworn.  As they heard the unmistakable sounds of the shutters being removed from the shop windows, the bookseller assured her, "I will bring him home."

Descending the stairs, Walter found Albert Medhurst's countenance to be uncannily similar to that of his housekeeper.  He offered the very same words, "I will bring him home."

Walter was aware that he had made a very grave promise to two people most dear to him.  It was a promise that he was not entirely certain that he could keep, yet he would give every morsel of his being to do so.  He left his bookshop enroute to the Criminal Court at Newgate, commonly referred to as The Old Bailey.  Shortly before ten o'clock in the morning, he found himself sitting in the court along with a diverse assortment of London citizens, all waiting anxiously for the trial to begin.

Some time around half-past ten, the court suddenly hushed.  John and three other boys were led to the prisoner's dock.  One of these other boys was approximately the same age as John, and two were much younger.

The officer of the court began by reading out a date and stating that on that date, "It is the contention of The Crown that all four of these boys, along with a fifth, killed in the action, conjured a plan to rob Mr. Walter Boniface, a bookseller from Westminster, of some valuable books that he was transporting.  John Kenworthy, James Grady, Samuel West and Joseph Black each stand charged with highway robbery.  The Crown contends that Samuel West and Joseph Black brandished knives and that each stole a book from the rearmost in the train of four carts.  Taking advantage of the confusion caused by their young accomplices, it is contended that James Grady and John Kenworthy put in fear the driver of the second cart in the train in the attempt to rob said cart, aided in this action by the deceased Charlie Ramsden.  The Crown further contends that during the course of this robbery, disagreement broke out between the robbers, leading to one of them being murdered by another, and that the one who committed the killing suffered a stab wound from a third.  In addition to highway robbery, John Kenworthy is also charged with murder, and James Grady with wounding."

The accusation being read, the judge announced, "The court will now hear the pleas of the accused."

John, being accused of the most serious crime, entered his plea first.  He pled not guilty to the charge of murder, and not guilty to the charge of highway robbery.  He did not stand charged with any other crime, but on the advice of his counsel, he admitted that he had conspired with James Grady and Charlie Ramsden to steal a single book from Mr.

Boniface.  The other three boys each entered a plea of *not guilty* on all charges.

The first witness to take the stand was the slippery officer from the Bow Street Runners, Constable Williams, who gave details on his investigation into the events of the day.  He stated his identity and was twice beseeched to speak in a lower tone of voice, a directive that he obeyed with great difficulty.  Sufficiently quieted, he explained how he had tentatively identified the dead thief as one *Charlie Ramsden* through a letter he had on his person.  Traveling to the address to which that letter had been sent, he had questioned the occupants therein, one of whom had blood visible upon his clothing.  One of the younger lads had blurted out that a boy named Charlie was missing from their company.  He then considered it confirmed that the letter in the possession of the dead boy was indeed his own.  Williams related the contents of the letter.  It was a reference and recommendation from a fishmonger with whom Charlie had previously been employed, but who had fallen on hard times and had been forced to dismiss the boy.

Constable Williams further explained that the boys found in the room closely matched the descriptions of those involved in the robbery, and that based upon this resemblance, he had made an arrest of the lot of them.  He explained that the landlord had sent him directly to John's place of employment at the bookshop, and that he had spoken to another bookshop employee to gather information before confronting the boy.  He advised the court that the injured John had confessed to a lesser crime in the presence of his employer.  He added that it was his belief that John had been entirely complicit in all aspects of the robbery.

John's counsel asked Williams to justify this final assertation, given that collected witness statements all agreed that John had defended his employer's property during the robbery.  The Bow Street Runner could not come up with convincing evidence, but he reasserted that he was confident of the boy's full complicity.

The second witness called to testify was one Mr. Walker, he being one of the two constables hired by Mr. Boniface on that fateful day. He recounted how he and his fellow constable had been distracted by the two younger boys, alleged to be Samuel and Joseph, after they had each snatched one book from the rear cart. He confirmed that the boys had escaped, and that he and his partner had recovered the stolen books that the boys had dropped in the street not at all far from the train of carts. He also confirmed that he had seen nothing of the primary action of the day, but only its aftermath.

After the hired constable stepped down, the carter who had been driving the second cart was called. He confirmed that he had observed John sitting on the footboard of the cart in front of him, and that he had been there since they left Great Prescot Street. He advised that John seemed nervous, looking around in all directions shortly before the robbery began. He described at length how his attention had been distracted by a commotion at the rear of the train and further explained that moments after this distraction, two boys had approached his cart from opposite directions, knives drawn. They had ordered him to step down from the footboard, and one of these boys had trivially wounded him. He also confirmed that John had jumped from the lead cart as these two robbers began their attack and that he had, from the very beginning, fought against them. Cross-examined by John's counsel, he confirmed that the young bookshop employee had never helped the attackers, not even for an instant, but had fought against them from the very first moment.

Next, Walter Boniface presented his witness statement. He confirmed that the two younger boys had run up to the rear of the last cart in which he was riding, cutting the canvas over the books and helping themselves to a volume each. He testified that when he tried to stop them, they did brandish their knives in his direction. Glancing to the prisoner's box and seeing two innocent-looking young faces weeping in fear, he quickly pointed out that he never felt threatened by their rather childish presentation of the weapons and that their ability to run off with a book apiece was a consequence of their quickness and not of any threatened violence.

The prosecutor asked Mr. Boniface the value of individual books in the collection, and he responded, accurately, that their value ranged from as much as one-hundred pounds to as little as a shilling or two.  The prosecutor also asked the value of the two books grabbed by the young boys.  Unfortunately, by chance, one of those books was of some considerable value and Mr. Boniface was forced to answer that their total value was of about five pounds when combined.

Next, Mr. Boniface was questioned by John's counsel.  The lawyer asked, "Sir, on the date in question, were you the victim of a highway robbery?"

"I was, although the property stolen was quickly recovered."

"In total, how many robbers were involved?"

"Four."

"Was John Kenworthy among their number?"

"No.  Master Kenworthy defended my property against the robbers, suffering a significant injury in the process."

John's counsel continued, "The boy that was killed, was he among the robbers?"

"Most certainly, he was."

"Was the accused, James Grady, among the robbers?"

"I was able to achieve only a fleeting glimpse of the robber who is suspected to have been James Grady, yet I think it probable that it was him.  Nevertheless, given the seriousness of this matter, I will not positively identify him."  The counsel asked nothing about the two young boys.

The case having been stated, the judge offered each of the accused an opportunity to defend himself.  Each of the two younger boys claimed that initially, the plan was for them to simply cause a ruckus at the back of the line of carts, but not to steal anything.  While everyone was looking at them, Charlie was supposed to approach the cart on which John was riding, and he would be handed a single book while everyone was looking the other way.  They stated that all three older boys, including John, had discussed this plan.  They further explained that early on the morning of the unfortunate event, after John had left for his job at the bookshop, James and Charlie had coerced them into carrying knives and stealing books from the rear cart, instead of just causing confusion.  They each confirmed that John knew nothing of this change of plans.

James Grady claimed that he had gone to the scene in a valiant and heroic effort to prevent the crime from taking place.  Evidence from all others at the scene that day entirely overwhelmed his creative lie, and, to his detriment, his untrue statement served to confirm that he was indeed present on the day.  It was rather sad to perceive his level of desperation, for the evidence against him was damning.

John told the story in much the same way as had the two young boys.  He admitted that he had been a willing participant in the plan to steal a single book, in no way denying his guilt in that conspiracy.  He did, however, adamantly deny that he planned, or was even aware of the highway robbery.  He insisted that he was expecting only to slip Charlie a single book while everyone else was looking away.  As to his actions once the violence began, he stated that he was protecting the assets of his employer who, at that point, stood to lose far more than a single volume.  When asked by the prosecutor what he thought would be the value of the volume that he intended to steal, John answered, "I do not know the exact value of the book I had chosen, but I think between ten and fifteen shillings."

John's own counsel walked up to him very deliberately and asked, "John Kenworthy, you have already confessed to being a party to a plan to steal a single book from your employer.  Do you swear here, before

Almighty God, that you did not know that the other boys were planning to alter that plan and instead commit a highway robbery?"

John responded, "I do swear, before God, that I was not aware."

The counsel continued, "And, Master Kenworthy, would you like to make any statement in regard to that crime of which you are guilty?"

Having obviously been coached in his answer to this question, John quite eloquently replied, "I have freely confessed my guilt for the attempted theft of a single book, but I am guilty of no other crime. I understand the seriousness of the crime that I did attempt. I have brought inexcusable shame upon myself, and I have wronged Mr. Boniface, a kind and generous man, for which I am very deeply sorry. When I observed the other boys committing a violent robbery, I never for a single moment had any other thought but to fight for Mr. Boniface's interests." His tears were real.

John's counsel continued, "As for Charlie Ramsden, he did die as a result of wounds that you inflicted. Did you intend to kill him?"

"I did not, Sir. That very morning, I would have called Charlie a dear friend. I so wish that I could have stopped the robbery without killing him, but he was on me at once with his knife drawn, and I had no choice but to fight him, both in self defense and to protect Mr. Boniface's property. I'm so very saddened that I inflicted fatal wounds on him, for that was never my intent."

Finally, John's counsel asked him, "Who was it that inflicted the wound upon you that day?"

"It was James Grady, Sir, just after I cut Charlie."

"And was he also attempting to rob from the carts at the time?"

"Yes, Sir, he was."

With that, the testimony ended, and the case was handed to the jury.

The jury deliberated for half an hour before returning a detailed verdict. The foreman read it to the court:

"We find that James Grady, Samuel West and Joseph Black are guilty of highway robbery. We do not recommend mercy for James Grady. We do recommend mercy for Samuel West and Joseph Black as we feel they were coerced by the older boys, and that they are very young and impressionable.

"We find that James Grady is also guilty of the wounding of John Kenworthy during the commission of the crime of highway robbery.

"We find that John Kenworthy is not guilty of murder in the killing of Charlie Ramsden, that being an act of defence against highway robbery. We find also that John Kenworthy did not take part in that highway robbery and is not guilty of that charge. By his own admission, he is guilty of conspiracy to steal a book from his employer. As to the value of the book that he intended to steal, we refer to Mr. Boniface's statement that the books being transported ranged in value from as much as one hundred pounds to as little as a couple of shillings. We shall therefore assume a value of one pound."

The justice thanked the jury and dismissed them. He then looked at the four occupants of the prisoner dock and shook his head. "What foolish actions by all of you." He paused and ominously donned his black cap. He then began again, "By way of sentence, James Grady, for your crimes, you shall suffer death by common hanging. May God have mercy upon your soul." After a brief pause, he continued, "The law does allow the imposition of the sentence of death, or of transportation for the crimes of Samuel West and of Joseph Black, but Our Saviour also entreats us to show mercy, especially to the very young. Masters West and Black, you shall each be confined in prison for three months, and you are hereby most gravely warned that if you ever in the future undertake similar actions, the gallows await." Turning at last to John, he said, "John Kenworthy, you betrayed the trust of your employer in arranging to deprive him of his property.  It is not lost upon the court that you also acted nobly on the behalf of that same employer in defending against a more serious loss.  You are guilty, by your own admission, of the crime of conspiracy to steal from your employer and shall be confined for three months.  As to any expenditure undertaken by Mr. Boniface subsequent to the crime, specifically his generous payment of your doctor's bill and your legal counsel, this is a civil matter and the gentleman has advised me that he does not wish to pursue that matter at this time, yet he shall have the right to pursue it in the future if he so chooses.  Bear the prisoners hence."

The court officers escorted the prisoners out of the dock.  Only James, the one sentenced to death, seemed unemotional.  He walked out with a blank expression while the other three, including the mature John Kenworthy, all had noticeable tears in their eyes.

Walter Boniface thought the judgement against John and the two young boys to be fair.  He would have very much preferred a sentence of transportation, rather than death, for James Grady and he planned to petition the court for clemency in that case.  He asked the officer if he could speak briefly with John and his request was granted in the entry-way just outside the court.  "John," he said kindly, "in three month's time when your sentence is completed, come to the shop.  I would still be proud to have you as an employee."  Looking at the two frightened boys beside him, he added, "And bring your young friends with you.  I think we can find some work for them as well."

"You are the kindest of gentlemen, Sir."  With that reply, John and the other prisoners were led to their respective fates.


Although it was some distance and hackney cabs were waiting, Walter Boniface decided to walk back to his shop.  He needed time to think about mercy and justice and how these two concepts were not often to be found in the same place.  To his manner of thinking, the kindness he bestowed upon John was entirely natural, yet he knew it to be rare in the world.  Walter had no children of his own, and was most unlikely indeed to ever have any, so he treated John almost like a son.  A good parent does not discard a son for some small transgression, and he did not intend to discard John.  It was possible to destroy young John Kenworthy for his error, and it was also possible to use the lesson of that error to help him to become a better man.  The Westminster bookseller could imagine no other course but to do the latter.

As he walked into the bookshop, Mr. Medhurst rushed to him.  Mrs. Hewitt, having been watching for his return from an upstairs window, made a rare appearance in the shop as well.  He gave both the generally good news, that John was to serve a three-month sentence, but that he had avoided the gallows.  He told them of his promise of employment to John and the two younger boys once their sentence was completed.  Finally, he asked Mr. Medhurst to continue minding the shop for a few minutes longer as there was one thing more that he needed to do.

Walter went upstairs to the little desk in his bedroom where he normally wrote his dream log.  At that desk, he penned a letter to the judge in that morning's trial.  He stated that he felt it his moral duty to suggest that young James Grady might be effectively reformed and may yet be of good service to Britain or her Empire.  This confidence compelled him to beg the court to commute James Grady's sentence of death to transportation.  He sent off his letter with the late post.

Two days later, a reply arrived from the judge.  In that terse reply, the judge stated that Mr. Boniface had justly performed his moral duty by begging for clemency, but that he must perform his duty as well.  The sentence of death would stand.

Before another week had passed, James Grady was hanged at Newgate.  That evening, prior to tending their own fires, the couple agreed that the world was in no way a better place for the death of a young man who had simply made one mistake.  They abhorred the loss, but they were simply a pair of molly booksellers from Westminster.  The world didn't care what they abhorred.

## Chapter 8 – An Absence and a Return

Over the next several weeks, the drear of winter took an even firmer hold on the great city.  It was wet and windy, although never cold enough for snow.  Mud and grime lined the streets and was tracked onto every inch of the floor, which needed to be swept several times each day.  Although he would never say it out loud, Walter thought to himself that Albert was not nearly so good a sweeper as young John.

In the gloom of the season and circumstance, there was a palpable air of unhappiness that permeated both professional and personal lives.

One morning in mid-December, Walter noted a brief obituary in the newspaper:

*Thomas Paynter, physician, late of The City, died Saturday last at Tottenham, aged 81.*

And that was all.  A lifetime of service to his fellow man summed up in a single bland sentence.  "So go we all," thought the bookseller sadly to himself.

The great majority of the old doctor's collection of books had been sold, with just a few of the less desirable volumes remaining among the shop's regular stock.  A procession of distinguished customers had visited, seeking out the rarer works, but that procession had ended.  Walter Boniface was a far wealthier man for his purchase of the library from Great Prescot Street, having reaped close to five-thousand pounds on an investment of only a tenth of that.  Yet it had come at a heavy cost.  He fretted daily over the wellbeing of young John, shut up in the dismal prison.

Walter and Albert continued their nightly discussions, and occasionally tended their own fires.  The strain of the odd situation, and of the season, touched them as well from time to time, and there were a few unkind words spoken.  There were no serious schisms, just occasional misplaced frustrations boiling to the surface.  Even Mrs. Hewitt was feeling the strain.  At her employer's encouragement, she had taken a week's leave from her housekeeping duties to visit her sister in Wool-wich.

Both booksellers continued to explore dreaming as an artform in and of itself.  Walter's familiar dream of John stealing a single shilling from a gushing cashbox recurred about once per week – it had become almost a joke between the friends.  He would simply say, "I lost another shilling last night," and his friend was thus informed that the dream had oc-curred once again.  Both men tried to find interpretation in this image, but both failed.

Albert, for his part, had experienced a lucid dream, that being one in which the dreamer is fully aware that the experience is a dream and can influence its progress, to some degree at least.  This made his friend just a bit jealous.  Walter had read of such a phenomenon but had never ex-perienced it himself, despite having been a dedicated dreamer for much longer than Albert.

Christmas Day came.  On that afternoon, Walter and Albert took a long walk along The Strand, through Temple Bar and down Fleet Street.  They proceeded onwards past St. Paul's Cathedral and out to the middle of London Bridge.  The Thames flowed entirely clear of ice.  It had been only several years since the 1814 frost fair, a merry event held on the frozen river where sellers set up stalls on the ice and a fine time was had by all.  That was until the ice suddenly broke up and many drowned.

On this afternoon, there was no ice to impede the progress of a small boat shooting the bridge on the outgoing tide.  The friends wondered what its mission might be on this, of all days.

There being nothing on the south side of the river that greatly inter-ested either man, they turned around in the middle of the bridge and walked back into The City.  Broadly retracing their footsteps, they returned, quite chilled, to the bookshop just ahead of the early midwinter sunset.

And so it went, through January and February.  Business was fair, even good at times, but there was a notable air of unhappiness in that little bookshop.  Both gentlemen thought daily about John, his misery and his safety, in that horrid prison.  His absence left a gaping hole in daily life, and it was felt deeply.

One frigid and blustery day when the new year was a couple of months old, the two men were tending the shop as they normally did.  The day had already seen a few customers and a couple of sales.  One man had brought in several older books in hopes of raising enough money to discharge a debt.  The books were of some age but were not in the very best condition and he declined to part with them for the price offered.  All in all, it had been a rather typical day.

The uneventful afternoon continued until about 2 o'clock when, suddenly, Albert Medhurst's face turned ashen.  "Oh, Walter…"  He pointed to the street in front of the store.  Through the window could be seen the most unkempt figure that had ever walked the streets of London.  His clothes were scarcely qualified to be called clothes at all, being more like mud- and blood-stained rags.  His face was filthy and bloodied, but it was also unmistakable.

Walter flew through the door.  "John!  My boy, welcome back!"  An equally filthy and somewhat younger boy stood with him.  "Samuel?" Walter said, hesitatingly, to that heap of soiled cloth.  The boy gave a scarcely perceptible nod.  "And where is the other boy, Joseph?"

"He's dead, Sir," replied John.  "Another prisoner stole his food, and he fought back.  He was beaten terrible.  Truly awful, Sir.  The turnkeys left him there bleeding on the floor 'till he died, wouldn't let us help him."

Walter was shocked by this news, and equally shocked by John's dispassionate description of the event.  He had no words.  He took the two surviving boys at once to Mrs. Hewitt so that she might help them to clean themselves up and make themselves presentable.  It would be a formidable task.  The housekeeper gave the boys some bread and cheese, which they consumed greedily before realizing their lack of manners.  She understood that they were starving and took no offence.  Later, Mr. Boniface sent her to the shops with some money to purchase new clothes for the boys, as they could not work in the torn rags that they had been wearing.  Before the shutters went up, the two miserable wretches who had appeared at the door were once again respectable-looking young men.

After the bookshop closed that evening, five people sat around a wooden table in the rooms above.  It was an assembly that would have been roundly criticized, vilified and censured by church, government and general society alike.  It consisted of two people that shared a heartfelt romantic love for each other, and who just happened to be both male.  One of these was an employee of the other and therefore considered by society to be of a lower class.  The group also consisted of the housekeeper in the employ of this man, breaking bread as an equal.  Rounding out the gathering were two boys who were orphans, and furthermore, convicted criminals just that day released from prison.  Most members of upright English society would have scorned Mr. Boniface, a gentleman and property owner, for keeping such company.

Walter Boniface took a different view.  He was thoroughly convinced that the assemblage was not wrong: society was wrong.  He could think of no group of people with whom he would prefer to share an evening meal.  The five would come to feel as much familial kinship as any more traditional family possibly could.  There were secrets, but do not families always hold secrets?  Those undisclosed things, the secrets that they kept, had no bearing on their work in the shop or on this evening's shared meal, and they did not warrant any consideration whatsoever.

When dinner was finished, Walter presented John with a small keyring containing two keys.  The first opened the shop.  He would be expected to arrive, with Samuel as his assistant, to remove the shutters each morning at the very specific time which he knew well.  The second key was also familiar to John.  It was the one which opened his room in Shelton Street.  "I kept up the rent while you were gone.  You will need someplace to sleep."

Both John and Samuel were dumbfounded.  Neither had any idea where they would sleep that night, although they expected it would be on some street corner in the cold of winter.  This was more than they could have dreamt.  Initially speechless, John finally stammered out, "Sir, you... you are being too kind to us."

"Actually, John," responded Walter, "I think that I am being just kind enough.  I need a dedicated employee who I can trust, and I know of no one who better fills that requirement than you.  You did once betray my trust John, and you paid a heavy price for that betrayal.  Now I demand that you be worthy of even more trust.  You will take on a greater role in the shop.  You will need to learn more about our inventory, you will need to work hard, and you will need to teach young Samuel here.  Do all this, and I will ensure that you come to have the knowledge you require to become a highly respected bookseller in your own right.  I can assure you, from personal experience, that it is a fine profession for one to hold."

Walter then turned his gaze to the younger boy.  "Samuel, you are about the same age that John was when he first came to me.  I need to be able to trust you as well.  I'm sure that you never want to see the inside of a prison again, do you?"

"No Sir, I do not," Samuel responded sheepishly, "I will work hard for you every day.  God bless you Sir."

Walter took Samuel's entreaty to God in the spirit that it was intended, even though he had little use for anything religious.  "Well then, Samuel, you will listen to John when he tells you what needs to be done around the shop and if you have any questions, just ask him, or me or Mr. Medhurst.  Don't interrupt any of us when we are dealing with customers and be careful with the books.  Some of them are worth a lot of money."

"I promise, Sir," replied Samuel sincerely.

The strange gathering, the bane of church and society alike, enjoyed the rest of their meal.  Afterwards, the two boys returned to the room in Shelton Street, which seemed more than a bit empty, or perhaps overcrowded with too many ghosts.  Nevertheless, it served them as warm shelter.  Mrs. Hewitt completed her duties and retired to her own personal pursuits.  Walter and Albert sipped gin and conversed well into the night.


Bright and early the next morning as Walter finished his last bite of breakfast, the shutters were being removed from the shop windows by young John, who was actively instructing younger Samuel in the process.  Mr. Medhurst had arrived a minute or so earlier but had decided to stop in the street for a few moments rather than interfere with John's duties.  The weather was still cold and there was a light icy drizzle in the air, but the spell of sadness that had seemed to hang over the little bookshop for the last several months had been lifted.  Even on that cold and dreary day, the store seemed to hold a warmth, and all of Walter Boniface's staff basked within it.

## Chapter 9 – As Family

John had returned on a Wednesday and by Saturday, it was as if he had never been gone.  As well as selling books (in significant numbers), he ran errands and all the while continued to coach Samuel in his duties.

The younger boy kept the shop swept clean and helped to organize books after customers had scattered them with their browsing.  He also assisted Mr. Hewitt with her housekeeping and cooking duties.  He had learned to be a shadow, never interfering with customers.  On those rare occasions when he was spotted, he presented a bright smile and pleasing countenance that never failed to charm any gentleman or lady.

It had been decided a day or two earlier, by universal agreement, that the boys would take their evening meals in Mr. Boniface's rooms.  Mrs. Hewitt would be given a minor rise in pay to compensate for the extra work and the two boys would submit a small amount of their income to cover costs… almost at least.  Mr. Medhurst would join them in the meal, although he had most often taken his evening meal with Walter for some time past.

Rather late on that Saturday afternoon, shortly before the closing hour, a rather unpromising customer entered the store.  Somewhat shabbily dressed, he glanced first at the lowest priced books in the shop.  By way of looks and nods, both Mr. Boniface and Mr. Medhurst declined to undertake his service, leaving the task to John.  "Is there any way in which I might assist you, Sir?" the young employee enquired.

"I seek writings that may enlighten me on the subject of witches and witchcraft," the man responded gruffly.

John asked a question that either of the more senior booksellers might have overlooked.  "Does Sir seek instructive books on such practices, or books relating to the art of recognizing and apprehending witches."

"The latter, absolutely!"

"Well then, sir, might I suggest this grand old volume."  John picked up an old, yet splendidly bound book entitled, *"The triall of witch-craft."*  He opened it to the title page, surreptitiously glancing at both the subtitle and the name of the author.  Armed with this bit of information, he continued, "In this volume, Mr. John Cotta details the correct, and erroneous methods of witch discovery."  The potential customer took the book and perused a few pages.

The two more senior booksellers were watching from the rear of the shop.  Mr. Medhurst, knowing this to be a book of higher value than most in the shop, took a short step forward to assist.  This was halted by the shop owner who whispered, "Let him have his go at it."

The poorly dressed customer asked, "Well then, for what price would this book be obtained?"

John was aware that while this book was older and in reasonably good condition, making it of some value, it was not an often-sought-after title.  It could be worth little more than two pounds.  Consequently, John replied to the customer, "The book would sell for eight pounds, Sir."

"Eight pounds?  Preposterous!" responded the customer.  "I shall offer four."

"My dear sir," replied John, "I shall have to confirm with my employer, but I suspect he might be willing to sell the book for six pounds.  It truly is worth eight, but it has been in our inventory for some weeks.  My employer may be motivated to sell, and you might be able to obtain it at a bargain.  Would you be willing to pay six pounds, should he agree?"  When he concentrated, John could speak with remarkable eloquence.

Living in a rough neighbourhood, he had rarely found it prudent to do so, yet this moment was an exception.

"Very well then," said the mysterious customer, grudgingly.  "Six pounds and not a penny more."

John replied, "I thank you sir.  If you would be so kind as to excuse me for a moment."  With this, he stepped not more than three yards to Mr. Boniface, who had obviously heard everything that had just been said.  The two now spoke at a whisper.

"Tell him he may have it for seven, but accept six and ten," whispered Mr. Boniface.  The pair exchanged a few more feigned whispers only as a show for the customer, for there was nothing more to be discussed.

Returning to the customer, John said, "I'm very sorry Sir, but my master says that he requires no less than seven pounds for this particular book, as it is a very old and rare title."

"It is robbery I tell you, but as I have no other option, I will pay.  I expect that it will at least be well wrapped for my taking."

"Certainly, it shall be, Sir."  Mr. Boniface stepped forward to assist with the financial transaction while John wrapped up the book.  The customer left with a very rare tome, albeit one seldom sought after.  He might have searched every bookshop in London and its environs, and far beyond as well, without finding another copy.  He paid a hefty price, but he left satisfied.  No one in the shop harboured any desire to ponder the question of why he was so preoccupied with witch-hunting.

With this lucrative last-minute deal, John's sales on the day exceeded those of the two senior booksellers combined.  He would receive a generous commission for his skillful handling of this customer.  None of them ever learned who the buyer truly was.  It was presumed that his unkempt wardrobe was a ruse intended either to feign poverty in hopes of securing a better deal, or to conceal his true identity for some unknown reason.  In either case, he had not counted upon encountering a salesman so cunning and skillful as young John Kenworthy.

By the time the transaction with the mysterious customer was completed, it was slightly past the normal closing hour.  As John and Samuel put up the shutters, Walter turned to Albert and said, "Do you now understand why I kept him on staff even after his trouble with the law?"  Albert had understood before, but this episode removed any doubt as to his friend's wisdom on the matter.


As the four climbed to the upstairs rooms, the most inviting aroma of roasting meat wafted down.  Mrs. Hewitt had truly outdone herself this evening.  She was serving roast leg of lamb, purchased at a very fair price from the market that morning.  Onions and potatoes along with fresh bread rounded out the meal.  The five cheerful people sat down around the wooden table in the kitchen and started at their dinner.

As time went by, the conversation ranged hither and yon.  At one point as the meal neared an end, Mrs. Hewitt gave a kindly look toward John and Samuel.  "Tomorrow is Sunday.  Are you boys planning to attend church services?"  The boys looked awkwardly at each other.  It was not that they objected to such an endeavour; they had simply never considered it.  Seeing their uncertainty, Mrs. Hewitt continued, "If you should wish it, I would be happy to escort you to the church that I attend and ensure that you feel comfortable in that place, and with the people around you."

John and Samuel looked at each other once again, as if confirming consensus, then John said, "Yes, Mrs. Hewitt, I think we would like that."

"Oh, I'm very happy to hear it."  She arranged a time and a place to meet the next morning in a small square close to the church.  She advised, "It is tradition to offer up some small amount of coin at the service to help support the church, if you are able.  It need not be much at all."  John stated that he would have no problem coming up with a contribution, having made many sales that week culminating with the most lucrative one scarcely more than an hour earlier.  He made it clear that his donation would be for both himself and Samuel.  After a bit more conversation, and the offering of help in cleaning up, John and Samuel departed for their room in Shelton Street.

Following the departure of the boys, Mrs. Hewitt turned to Mr. Boniface.  "Sir, I hope I didn't overstep my boundaries in inviting the boys to attend church with me.  I know that you yourself have little interest in that institution."

Walter smiled and replied, "Mrs. Hewitt, neither you nor the boys are in my employ on a Sunday.  It is not for me to say how you, or they, should pass the time on that day.  You are most kind in your offer to escort them."  Secretly, he was thinking that the boys worked so hard six days per week that they should have the seventh to simply be boys, but he kept this opinion to himself.


That evening over glasses of gin, Walter read his dream log to Albert.  As fascinating as it was, it was largely a rehash of previous night's themes, simply reshuffled for a new dawn.  He did, however, recall a small part of the dream that he had not recorded in writing.  He described it from memory: "I dreamt that you, my dearest Albert, and I were walking down The Strand as a couple, hand in hand for all to see, just as many a man and woman do every day."

Albert smiled at this.  It was such a beautiful concept.  He even felt a single tear welling up in his eye is he imagined taking such a stroll with Walter.  "What a wonderful vision.  It's so sad that we know it never can be."

Walter replied, "I do regret that we ourselves shall not have that privilege in our lifetimes, but perhaps those of our nature yet to be born will someday enjoy this simple pleasure."

"Well, I envy them," Albert responded sincerely. "To walk down the street as we are, in love, proud and gay. That is truly an experience worthy of dreams. How sad that we can't even record such dreams in our private logs for fear of being found out."

Walter suggested, "Might I offer a simple code for recording dreams of this most agreeable kind in our logs. Let's just include, as a sentence unto itself, the single word, *'Dreamt.'*"


The following morning, John and Samuel met with Mrs. Hewitt at the appointed time in a little square opposite a small church. Each of the boys had taken some extra time to wash and make himself presentable for the special occasion. "Oh, it's so good to see you this morning, boys!" beamed Mrs. Hewitt. "Come now, let us go inside. I arrive early as I perform some small volunteer efforts in assisting the verger, the churchwarden and the sexton on Sunday mornings, and I also offer help in the vestry before the vicar arrives." The boys were not quite sure what language she was speaking, yet they followed her anyway.

As the start of the service drew near, the three sat together in the appropriate pew. Mrs. Hewitt whispered to the boys, "We shall be hearing today a sermon by the Reverend Mr. Hillyard. Take heed at what he has to say for it may save your souls." Until this day, John and Samuel had never been instructed in religion and therefore did not know that their souls were in peril. John had read a bit about Christianity and the Church of England, but the subject had never enthralled him sufficiently to encourage any detailed study. The younger boy knew almost nothing of religion.

Both boys tried to follow the flow of the sermon, but each found it generally bewildering. The reverend habitually referenced verses from the bible. John had been read some small portions of the bible by his late mother many years earlier, but he was by no means well-versed. Samuel was aware that the holy book existed, but little more. The Reverend seemed sincere, but his words furnished the boys with little elucidation.

Following the sermon as they walked outside of the church, Mrs. Hewitt asked them if they found the sermon inspiring.  The boys, by their nature, were both polite and honest and these traits conflicted.  Consequently, they did not answer verbally.  In their awkward shuffling and reluctance to speak, Mrs. Hewitt had her reply.  "Oh well, that's alright.  This is all new to you.  There is a bible school available to attend on Sunday afternoons.  It can teach you more about the Church of England and our beliefs.  Are you interested in attending?"

Neither John nor Samuel wanted to be unkind to a woman who had been so very kind to them, but in fact, they were most decidedly not interested in attending.  After an awkward pause, John replied, "We will consider the offer, Mrs. Hewitt, for future Sundays.  Today however, we have other matters to which we must attend."

"Well boys, I can't imagine what those matters might be on the Lord's Day, but I do wish you all the best."  With that, she took her leave of them.

As the boys walked, Samuel inquired of John, "The man said we must repent our sins.  What does that mean?"

John explained the concept to the best of his ability.  "It means that we must pray to Jesus and tell him that we are sorry for the evil things we have done, and we must accept his forgiveness."  The explanation was an imperfect summation of the views of the Church of England given by one with no formal religious education, but it was not catastrophically off its mark.

Samuel thought about this.  "We were in prison for three months.  Didn't we show we were sorry then?"

"No, Samuel, they are different things.  We didn't go to prison for our sins, but for our crimes.  Crimes are offences against men while sins are against God."

"So, it's not a sin to steal, but only a crime?"

"That's not it.  Stealing is a sin as well, but Jesus can forgive us if we let him."

Samuel was still confused, as was his instructor.  "You said Jesus will forgive us, but you also said that sins were offences against God.  Who do we pray to if we want to be forgiven, God or Jesus?"

John explained with a level of comprehension similar to that of an average Christian.  "God and Jesus are the same, but separate.  They are the father and the son, but they are also the same person.  And there is another part called the Holy Ghost."

"A ghost?" said Samuel mockingly.  "You're putting me on."  The two boys decided to abandon the discussion of religion for the rest of the day.

Back in the rooms above the shop, Walter and Albert were preparing the Sunday evening meal.  John and Samuel would be on their own this evening, so the meal was for just three.  Walter had borrowed a book on modern cooking from the shop and he related to Albert an innovative idea contained within that book.  This recipe was such a magnificent concept that he thought it might one day revolutionize gastronomy in England, and around the world.  It was a type of food whose invention was anecdotally (albeit rather dubiously) attributed to an earl whose holdings were located in the county of Kent, southeast of London.  This earl wanted to be able to eat a meal without interrupting his cribbage game.  He had therefore requested that his servants bring him a piece of meat placed between two slices of bread, so that he may pick it up and eat it without utensils.

Albert was intrigued by Walter's description of this new gastronomical miracle.  "My word," he blurted, "that is so simple yet so ingenious.  Double bread with meat!"

"Hmmm," Walter replied, "That might be one name for it, but as the individual credited with its invention was the Earl of Sandwich, it has come to be known as a *sandwich*.  We have lamb yet uneaten from last night, and bread as well, so I shall combine them to make sandwiches for this evening's meal."  Eventually, Mrs. Hewitt returned from some later-than-normal volunteer work at the church and all three enjoyed the novel dinner recipe.

Once the meal was completed, the dishes washed up and the kitchen made tidy once again, Mrs. Hewitt prepared to retire to her room, but Mr. Medhurst ask if she might join them in the parlour for a few moments.  She was offered a bit of gin and as was her custom, she took great exception to the offer, then readily accepted it.  Albert spoke to both companions, "You know Mrs. Hewitt that Mr. Boniface and I often compare dreams that we have experienced in the night.  I thought it might amuse you to hear of one of mine from last night."  All took a sip then he continued, "We all know that the late King George III was quite mad for the last years of his life."

Mrs. Hewitt, having consumed no more than a couple of sips of gin, interrupted Mr. Medhurst, commenting with slurred speech, "Confidentially, I think his successor to be at least as mad."  She apparently had a very low tolerance for alcohol.  "And his true queen, how he treated poor Caroline and put her in her grave.  Oh, that such a man should rule us."  She stopped her rant as quickly as she had begun it.

Mr. Medhurst continued, "At any rate, in my dream I saw the coronation of last summer, but in the carriage was not our new King, George IV, but instead, you Mrs. Hewitt, all bedecked in robes of ermine."

The housekeeper laughed heartily at this, "Me!  To be coronated Queen?  Oh, dreams are such silly things!"  All were laughing merrily.

Albert continued, "I do know, Mrs. Hewitt, that your given name is Elizabeth, and of course we once had a Queen Regnant by the name of Elizabeth."

"Ay, that we did," she laughed, "but very long ago.  I think the age of fe-male rulers to be long past.  There will surely never be another monarch named Elizabeth.  If a king today cannot find a male heir in the belly of his wife, I think he shall find one born to a mistress."  Another hearty laugh from the housekeeper.

"Well, Mrs. Hewitt," continued Albert, "you looked positively splendid in the Carriage of State riding away from Westminster Abbey."

Mr. Boniface commented, "Times are changing with every passing day, Mrs. Hewitt.  Perhaps, one day, we shall have another monarch named Elizabeth, or one with some other female name."

"Well, Sir, that will be a different day.  Oh, my head is all swimming.  Having been crowned, I must now go to bed.  A fine goodnight, gentle-men."

All three occupants of the room rose, and Mr. Medhurst held open the parlour door as the housekeeper staggered through.  He could not resist bowing slightly and saying, "Your Majesty," as she left the room.  Mrs. Hewitt would sleep well that night.  From her room, moments later, rang out the lyrics of, 'God Save the… *Queen*,' a song never before sung.

Walter laughed.  "Albert," he said, "Remind me of this night if I ever again offer my housekeeper anything more than the tiniest sip of gin."

"I fear that I am to blame," Albert conceded through a muffled laugh.  "I wanted to tell her of my dream of her coronation.  Perhaps discussion of dreams is something we should keep to ourselves."

"Well, she enjoyed the evening to be sure.  But I doubt that she will re-member it.  What other images did you record in your log last night?"

"There was one part of the dream," Albert replied,  "that I found rather disturbing.  In a room that I did not recognize, there were two men.  One appeared to be that ill-clad gentleman from yesterday afternoon to whom John sold the expensive book.  The other I did not know, nor do I recall his face.  They approached one another and as they came face to face, strange growths appeared upon their shoulders.  The first man grew an appendage that resembled a very large pitcher plant, whereas the other man produced a second head like that of a snake, small and misshapen, covered with mucus.  One man said to the other, 'Our monsters need to talk.'  With that, there seemed to be some parley between the abominations growing from their shoulders.  One of the monsters, I know not which, looked at me and said, 'Why is it that this man can see us, and remember us…,'  and it then identified what they, the monsters, were called.  I recall the identification to have been of two words in length, and I remember that in the dream I did not understand the meaning of the words spoken.  To my sadness and despite much thought, I cannot recall what the words were.  With this, the 'monster' on the unrecognized man's shoulder, that being the snake, detached and slithered into an adjacent room.  This phase of the dream then ended, or at least my memory of it ended."

Walter raised his eyebrows.  "I take it, Albert, that you were viewing this as an outside party.  I mean that in the dream, you were neither one of the men, nor one of the monsters."

"That is correct.  And additionally, I had the sensation throughout that I had somehow arranged this meeting, although I cannot explain the reasoning behind my coming to believe this."

Walter expressed his view on this unexplained knowledge.  "In dreams, we are sometimes simply aware of some fact without knowing the reason for which we are aware.  Perhaps the knowledge comes from parts of the dream that we forget before awakening, or perhaps it comes directly from that part of our mind which is responsible for the authorship of such narratives.  Whatever the source, in dreams, we sometimes simply *know*, without evidence.  What I find most interesting is that you are aware that there was a name or identifying term shared between the monsters, even to the point of knowing that it consisted of two words, yet you are unable to recall these words."

Albert asked, "But Walter, monsters growing out of men?  What could it possibly mean?  In the dream, I felt no sense of recognition as to what the monsters might represent."

Walter needed only a moment to think.  "Surely the monsters are the central characters in this narrative.  Your mind put little effort into creating the images of the men.  One was a recent, somewhat mysterious customer whose image was fresh in your mind.  Would I be correct in speculating that you can tell me absolutely nothing of the appearance of the other, and that you recall only a blank face?"

"I think that would be an accurate assessment."

 "I thought as much.  But you saw the monsters in great detail.  Truly Albert, a pitcher plant?  That took some feat of imagination.  I cannot say that I have ever heard or read any stories depicting a monster that looked like a giant pitcher plant.  The mucus-covered snake is a common enough image from tales of terror, but unlike the men, you do recall it clearly.  When you can clearly describe characters from a dream, these characters are central to the narrative.  They are the ones in whose creation your mind has expended the greatest effort."

Albert raised his eyebrow, even though it was likely not an observable act in the dim candlelight.  "So, what do you think my pitcher plant and my slimy snake represent?"

"I think, Albert, that there are countless possible interpretations."

"Therein lies the problem," responded Albert.  "With nearly infinite possible interpretations, I can find no message in the imagery.  If you had dreamt such a dream, Walter, how would you interpret it."

Walter thought for another moment before explaining, "If I'd dreamt that dream, I likely would have seen the two monsters as representing the Christian faith and the government of this nation in their roles as givers of laws, including those laws that forbid our love.  I would not be able to tell you which monster represents which, but I think it monstrous that our love should be forbidden.  If a law or edict is viewed as monstrous, then it might be represented in dreams as an actual monster.  Perhaps your interpretation would not include Christianity since you, unlike me, continue to hold religious beliefs.  Or, as a Roman Catholic, perhaps one of the monsters might represent the more powerful Church of England."

Albert took a long sip, very nearly emptying his glass.  "I do cling to my family's Catholic faith, and I hope of a merciful creator, yet as to the opinions of either my faith or those of the Church of England that would gladly see us hanged, I am as hostile as you.  If love is indeed a gift from God, then why does he give us love for one another but then adjudge it to be abhorrent?"  Walter had no answer to this question, and his dear friend was not actually expecting one.  "Oh, I think I've had enough of men and monsters.  It is all too much for tonight.  There will be other evenings."  Albert consumed the very last sip of his gin, then the two gentlemen rose from their chairs and descended the stairs.  Walter watched until his friend was safe inside the building containing the cobbler shop, then retired to his own bedroom.  He slept well again that night.

## Chapter 10 – Evolution

The mornings came and the evenings went.  Six days per week, Mrs. Hewitt prepared breakfast and shortly after, John and Samuel removed the shutters, right on queue.  Customers entered and left.  Business was profitable, if not lucrative.  Early in the evening, meals were enjoyed, and later in the evening, Walter and Albert enjoyed one another's company.

During business hours, Young Samuel energetically cleaned and organized the shop, then repeated the task.  While he would also occasionally run simple errands and assist Mrs. Hewitt, it could not fail to be recognised that at least a portion of his labour was merely for show.  The shop, as he started to clean and organize it for the third time on any given day, had not accumulated any detectable grime or disorganization since he had performed his task for the second time.

One night during their habitual discussions over glasses of gin, Walter had offered to allow Albert to hire the young boy away for part of the next day so that he might perform his tasks of cleaning and organization in the room over the cobbler.  On that day, after Samuel had completed his first circuit of maintaining the bookshop, Mr. Medhurst took him up the street to his room for the purpose of instructing him on the duties he was expected to complete at that location.


The pair had only just left the bookshop when a stout carriage stopped outside.  Mr. Boniface observed a respectable looking, albeit very large gentleman being assisted out of the carriage and thereafter, through the door of the bookshop.  The man was great both in height and girth and it was only with difficulty that he negotiated the narrow aisles between stacks of books.  He called out from just inside the door, "I trust your floorboards to be sturdy and capable of bearing my great weight."

In all the years Walter Boniface had operated the bookshop, this had never, on any previous occasion, been the first concern of a customer. He replied, "I am quite certain that they are up to the task, my good Sir," although given the immense size of the individual, it was prudent to entertain some small doubt.

Accompanying this imposing gentleman was a boy of perhaps ten or eleven years of age, also dressed in a respectable manner. The boy's eyes darted quickly over the selection as if seeking out some specific subject matter. He had completed two entire laps of the shop before the imposing older gentleman had reached the centre. John tried to assist him, but even that wiry young man could not keep up. With little delay, the enthusiastic boy focused upon works relating to the natural sciences, including zoology, botany and geology.

The substantial gentleman inquired as to the availability of some obscure medical books relating to research on the eyes. The shop owner, sadly, had to disappoint him as he had no such books in stock. "However," he said, "if Sir would like to leave an address at which he might be contacted, I shall make enquiries in an effort to obtain these works."

"That presents difficulties," rumbled the gentleman, "as I am in London only for a short time. I reside at Shrewsbury in Shropshire, some great distance from here, on the borders of Wales. But I shall leave my card and if you should come into possession of any of these works, do advise me by post." The gentleman handed Mr. Boniface a card that identified him as Robert Darwin, physician. Gesturing toward the boy's last known location, he continued, "And this excitable lad is my son, Charles." The gentleman then turned to his son and asked, "Have you found anything that might enhance our library."

"Indeed, I have, father," replied the boy, "several books."

"Well do bring them to me here, for you know that I move about as little as possible." Charles scurried about collecting a selection of books that had caught his eye on his first several orbits amongst the inventory. He quickly brought these volumes to the centre of the shop for his father's inspection.  That gentleman sorted them into two piles, accepting some and rejecting others.

John, being as helpful as possible, suggested a nicely bound and rather expensive two-volume work entitled *Zoonomia*.  Charles laughed at this suggestion and even the rotund and normally dour father appeared slightly amused.  The gentleman spoke directly to John, saying, "That is an excellent suggestion my lad, but I already own a copy of that book.  It was written by my late father."

Some minutes later, John and Mr. Boniface had finished wrapping up a dozen or so books.  Following a significant financial transaction, the great gentleman rotated on the spot and lumbered out the front door.  A footman assisted him into his large and sturdily built carriage.  Young Charles completed a circumnavigation of the vehicle, apparently undertaken for no purpose other than to fill the time while his father was being loaded.  At length, the boy jumped in.  Thanks to a great effort on the part of two hefty horses, the juggernaut started back toward The City.

Mr. Boniface flashed an approving look toward John, confirming that he had performed well during the unusual transaction.  Following this, both returned to the mundane tasks of keeping the shop organized and prepared for all customers, great and small.


Walter Medhurst had exited from the door adjacent to the cobbler shop just in time to see this carriage move away.  He caught a glimpse of the great man inside, and of the boy already removing the wrappings from one of the books.  Re-entering the shop, he was given details on what had just transpired, which he found amusing (although somewhat disappointing as well, as his absence had deprived him of a potential share of the commission.)

Mr. Medhurst turned to John and handed him two keys.  He explained, "These are duplicate keys to my room – you know which shop it's over.

The larger opens the door to the street whereas the smaller gains entry to the room itself.  Would you put them on your key ring so that you may allow Samuel to use them on days when he is given the task of cleaning my room.  I would prefer that you hold them and lend them to Samuel only for use on required occasions"

"Certainly, I shall keep them safe, Sir," John promised, and he added the keys to the ring that already held the key to his room in Shelton Street and the one that he used to open the bookshop each morning.  When sufficient time had passed for Samuel to complete his duties, Mr. Medhurst retrieved him and returned him to the service of the bookshop.  The young boy cleaned and organized in that establishment until the day's business ended.

Dinner was prepared by Mrs. Hewitt and enjoyed by all.  Later that evening after the boys had returned to Shelton Street, Walter and Albert conversed in the parlour.  Walter observed, "You place great trust in John by giving him your duplicate keys."

"I trusted him before the incident," Albert replied.  "But I think that I trust him even more now.  He erred, and now he wishes to atone for that error.  I share in your wish to allow him to atone.  But enough of business matters.  You have been eying that little journal of yours.  What do you have to tell me of last night's dreams?"

"Last night, I journeyed to America, my friend."

"And returned in time for breakfast," observed Albert lightheartedly as he took his first sip of gin.  "Dreams do hold great power indeed."

"Yes, but little in the way of clear instruction," cautioned Walter.  "I was at a seaport somewhere in England although I know not where.  The ship was at the wharf, and I saw crates and other goods being loaded.  I never recall boarding but suddenly, I found myself on the ship.  We were asea in a storm.  For some strange reason, I stood at the prow taking the full force of the gale, yet I didn't seem to get wet.  There was lightning and thunder, torrential rain and waves crashing over the deck, and I stood there observing it all, completely dry.  The ship then crested a great wave, and suddenly it was gone.  I inexplicably found myself in New York, in the United States on a street not entirely unlike one that we might see in London.  There were people, horses and shops with all the noise and commotion that we see here.  It was nighttime, but the streets seemed strangely lit, as if by thousands of lanterns."

"How did you know it to be New York?" asked Albert.

"I recall no outward evidence but, in my dream, I simply knew.  I saw a bookshop, and, out of professional curiosity, I entered.  It looked entirely different than our little shop; many times larger with stacks of books nearly as far as the eye could see.  I picked up one book and a rough-looking man, he appeared to be a navvy or something similar, rushed over and asked what I wanted with it.  I told him that I wanted to buy it, and I recall thinking the price very high, yet I paid it anyway.  As I turned to leave the great shop, I could not find the door.  I felt trapped in a maze of books, stacked higher than I could see over.  The books then transformed into a mature wood, full of oak, elm and pine trees.  I could not find my way out of this either but at length, I came to a small clearing.  Suddenly, there was John."

"Allow me to guess," interjected Albert.  "Did he steal a shilling again?"

"Gushing cashbox and all, in a clearing in the forest," responded his friend with a smile.  Scarcely a week went by without this image cropping up in Walter's dreams.  "Then, in an instant, I found myself back in our own shop and the dream ended."  By this time, the glasses had been drained and Walter rose to refill them.  After poking at the fire for a few seconds, he asked, "So, what do you think of all this, my friend?"

"Was this your first time in America?" asked Albert, obviously referring to journeys taken while asleep as he knew that his friend had never, in body, left England.

"It is the first time that I have been certain to be in America, although I have had some dreams where I was unsure where I might be and considered the possibility of being in that land.  I'm more curious about my odd sea voyage; how I stood in a tempest yet remained dry.  What do you think my mind might be suggesting with this image?"

After a moment's thought, Albert suggested, "Perhaps it's a demonstration of your belief that you may weather any storm and come through unscathed.  Your mind may have chosen a literal storm to represent metaphorical ones that you might successfully endure."

This speculative answer gave Walter pause.  He then inquired, "Isn't there a story in the bible about a man dreaming that he was on a ship during a storm?"

Albert thought for a moment, then replied, "You are probably referring to the story of Jonah, but that is not presented as a dream.  That is said to have actually happened."

"Didn't he go overboard and get swallowed by a whale?"

"It was a great fish," replied Albert.

"Either way, it sounds a lot like a dream to me.  I wonder how many of the sanctified stories of religion are simply distorted retellings of the dreams of long-dead men."

"Well, probably at least a few," conceded Albert, in spite of his continued adherence to at least a vestige of faith.


At that moment, there was a great commotion in the street. Cries of "Stop!  Thief!" were heard.  Walter and Albert sprang to their feet and pressed their faces to the parlour window.  What appeared to be a gentleman and a lady were present in the street a short distance away to their left, and a young person was seen running toward the right. Quickly, two other men sprang from an alleyway and apprehended the fleeing individual.  One of these men was tall and silent, the other much shorter but quite loud indeed.  While the taller one held onto the boy, the shorter yelled, "Consider yourself in custody!"  He then yelled louder than might have been thought necessary to the lady and gentleman only some seventy or eighty yards away, saying he was a constable and beckoning them over.

It was too dark to see the constable's face, but by his voice, there could be no doubt.  This was the slippery Williams of the Bow Street Runners who had, some months earlier, come to apprehend John.  His partner, judging by his tall stature and lack of voice, could only be Johnson.

In the street, Williams asked the gentleman, "This is the thief then?  What did he steal?"  That gentleman answered in a subdued voice that Walter and Albert could not hear from the upstairs window.  Fortunately, for the benefit of the inquisitive, Williams repeated and amplified everything that was said; "He stole a handkerchief, you say.  How much is it worth?"  "About six shillings, very good."  "Johnson, does he have a handkerchief on his person?"  "He does."  "Sir, is this your handkerchief?"  "It is…"  The official communications went on for a few minutes longer, then the voice of Constable Williams slowly faded off into the distance.

"Well, Albert," said Walter, "It's good to see that the constables from Bow Street are still protecting us."

In the parlour above the bookshop, the two friends sat down again.  "A bit sad, really," observed Albert.  "That wretched boy will probably be going to Australia for seven years, if not longer.  Most likely, he was just trying to survive."  To his surprise, Walter looked quite upset by this observation.  Albert realized that in this boy, his friend saw an echo of his own young employees and what they might have become had he not acted on their behalf.  He said, soothingly, "You can't save them all, Walter."

The hour being somewhat late, and the streets being safe on account of Constable Williams having frightened off every potential thief in all of Westminster, Albert decided that it was time to go home.  After a brief embrace, he departed for the night and made the short trek to his

unassuming room where he spent another night alone, as was man-
dated by the society in which he lived.

## Chapter 11 – A Letter for Mr. Medhurst

If Walter Boniface dreamt at all that night, then those dreams were of insufficient interest to warrant an entry in his log. He did, however, oversleep. Breakfast soon to be on the table, Mrs. Hewitt gently rapped at his bedroom door to remind him of the hour. For one as punctual as he, sleeping late was a very unusual occurrence.

Washing, shaving and dressing at double speed, he made up some, but not all, of the time lost to sleep. Breakfast was a hurried affair, and he was still running late. The last shutter had been stowed and the shop was up and running before the owner came downstairs. There was even a customer in the store who Mr. Medhurst was ably serving as John organized the inventory. Samuel had swept half of the floor, but as was shop policy, he had stopped and faded into the background when the customer had come in. Upon seeing his employer enter, the young boy picked up a small stack of letters stored near the cashbox. Handing these to Mr. Boniface, he received and appreciative smile in recognition of his fine work. The shop owner retreated to his private office to read the morning's correspondence.

Despite stepping out of the office from time to time, Walter spent the great majority of the morning in that private space while Albert Medhurst and John earned some respectable commissions. Very late in the morning, or perhaps it was just after noon, he re-entered the shop and approached Mr. Medhurst. The pair spoke quietly for a minute or so, then the senior bookseller called out, "John, we will be in my back office for a few minutes. If any of my favourite customers come in, call me. You can deal with the normal customers." With that, the pair disappeared into the cloistered chambre which the junior employees seldom glimpsed.

John knew exactly what Mr. Boniface meant by the term, '*favourite customers*.' Certainly, if an aristocratic-looking lady or gentleman should enter the store, then this individual would qualify as a favourite.  But an even more favoured customer would be one who was adjudged to be the servant of such a person.  Such a servant was likely to be delivering a request from his master in consideration of either the sale or purchase of valuable books.  Unfortunately for Mr. Boniface, no such servant arrived while the gentlemen were in the office, although John did ring up one modest sale to a *'normal customer.'*

When the two emerged from the office, Mr. Medhurst said to Samuel, "Get your hat, young man.  We are going over Westminster Bridge to see an architect about acquiring some books."  The young boy excitedly complied and the two stepped outside.  Within a few minutes they had been successful at hailing a cab.  They stepped into the cab and were gone, leaving Mr. Boniface and John to mind the store.

Still in the earlier part of the afternoon, not so very long after the pair had ridden off, one customer (who might or might not have qualified as a favourite) was being served by the bookshop owner.  As they negotiated the price of one or another historic volume, an officious-looking man entered the shop.  From behind a waxed moustache and while waving a cane somewhat dangerously, he enquired of John if one Mr. Albert Medhurst was employed therein.  "He is employed here, Sir," acknowledged John, "but he is currently away from the premises.  He is expected to return before the end of the day."

"I have a letter for that gentleman, of a personal nature," the self-confident messenger explained.  "Might I leave it with you for delivery?"

"Of course, Sir," replied John, "I would be more than happy to ensure that he receives it."  John placed the letter safely in the inner pocket of his jacket.  With a nod of his head and a huff, the man departed.

Over the next two hours there came into the bookshop a steady stream of customers.  Many made purchases, a few did not, and one lady sold a couple of books to Mr. Boniface.  Of all afternoons that Mr. Medhurst and Samuel should be absent, this one was rather ill-chosen as their aid would have been invaluable.  However, this surfeit of customers could in no way have been foreseen, and it was appreciated, despite the shortage of staff.  The shop owner and his junior assistant provided the best service that they possibly could, and each made a significant number of sales.

Eventually, Mr. Medhurst and Samuel returned with two crates of books.  These included many older and somewhat rare volumes that would likely fetch well over a pound each.  Mr. Boniface said to his friend with an air of confidence, "I trust you attained these at a most excellent price, Mr. Medhurst?"

"Well, Mr. Boniface, let's simply say that I purchased them for as low a price as I could possibly negotiate.  The seller was not some elderly doctor disposing of his collection in desperation, but rather a shrewd investor who demanded a goodly portion of their actual worth.  Nevertheless, I think there remains a healthy profit to be realized from our sale of these books."

After so many customers had traipsed through the shop that day, it was sorely in need of sweeping.  Samuel saw to that directly.  As seems to happen with startling regularity, once additional staff was available, the flow of customers all but stopped.  Mr. Boniface and John sorted through the newly acquired books noting those which would likely earn the most significant profit.

In addition to the large number of good-quality volumes, the lot included about six bibles, cheaply bound and in somewhat sadder condition.  Referring to these, Mr. Boniface instructed John to, "Put them in general stock for six shillings.  We will let them go for five each."

John looked at one of these, perhaps the one in the saddest condition of all.  He satisfied himself that it was missing no pages, then he said, "Sir, I would offer three shillings for this one."

Mr. Boniface was slightly surprised.  "They are five at minimum, John. But as you are a valued employee, I will reduce that to four in your case."

"But, you see, Sir, the binding is cracking, and this quire is loose…"

"Oh, very well, you may have it for three."  Walter momentarily thought, 'he has just stolen a shilling from me,' but then dismissed this thought.  John had stolen nothing but had ably negotiated to his own advantage.  He smiled at the boy and said, "I've made a fine negotiator out of you John!"  The purchase was recorded, and the bill of sale issued.

Before very long, the business day ended, the shutters went up and a meal was enjoyed at the wooden table in the kitchen.  John and Samuel left for Shelton Street and soon thereafter, Walter and Albert left for the latter's room over the cobbler shop.


The boys, too, were beginning to develop an evening routine.  Before the terrible incident that resulted in their incarceration, there had been five boys living in the room.  Three were older and they had little inter-action with the younger ones.  John was now the last survivor of the older boys, and tragically, little Joseph was gone as well.  The two survivors had passed terrible days together while incarcerated and had grown much closer.  John had taken on the role of an older brother to Samuel, and he found that he rather enjoyed that function.

John was teaching Samuel how to read.  It would not be accurate to say that Samuel was entirely illiterate, but his skills needed honing.  Until that day, instruction had taken advantage of discarded newspapers as reading material.  John's three-shilling bible would offer a new reading experience, and an opportunity to study the scriptures, all at once. Their lessons could become far more enlightening.

That evening, the pair had been reading the opening passages of The Book of Genesis when John paused for a moment to take off his jacket. "Oh, confound it!" he said as he suddenly saw the letter for Mr. Medhurst, which was still in the inside pocket. He had intended to deliver it to its addressee before the shop closed for the day, or at the very least before the end of dinner. Unfortunately, he had forgotten. "Samuel," he said, "I've been silly and forgotten to give a letter to Mr. Medhurst. I'll run it over to him now and come back in a short time." With that, he left the younger boy at Shelton Street and ran to the room above the cobbler shop.

When John arrived at the building in which Mr. Medhurst's kept his room, he used the larger key on his ring to open the door leading from the street. Proceeding up a stairway shared by several of the building's tenants, he knocked at the appropriate door. There was no reply.

Inside, Walter and Albert were tending their own fires and did not hear the knock. Their expression of affection for each other was not unlike that of many a man and woman in that, or any other city on that night, except in one aspect. They were not a man and a woman, but rather two men. All else was the same; they were equally in love.

In the joy of that moment, the knock at the door sounded like the footsteps of neighbours upon the stairs. It sounded like the din of the cobbler's hammer as he worked late. It sounded like the clatter of horses' hooves upon the street. It sounded like any of a thousand other sounds that might be heard in a large city such as London. It was not inaudible; it simply went unnoticed.

When John received no reply to the knock, he tried again. He once again was unheard. Now convinced that the resident was not at home, he located the smaller key on his keychain. He thought to leave the letter in a prominent place upon Mr. Medhurst's writing desk so that it might be seen as soon as the gentleman returned. He inserted the key into the lock. He opened the door.

By the light of a single candle and a well-tended fire, John saw his employer and the junior partner in the business, both quite naked, in an intimate position.

For the many thoughts that passed through his mind in the span of little more than a second, John was in no way to blame.  He could only interpret the sight that he had seen by the values of the society that encompassed him.  His interpretation was channelled narrowly by all that had ever been related to him from his youngest days.  John was not to blame for the revulsion he felt at that moment.  He could not be blamed for his confusion.  On that evening, in that second, John was wholly innocent of any wrong thought for he had no thoughts of his own.  He only echoed what every person he had ever known had taught him.  He was repulsed and horrified by Walter Boniface and Albert Medhurst lying together.  He could only interpret what he had witnessed as a most unnatural crime.  He dropped the letter and staggered back in shock.

"John, Wait…" Walter Boniface called out, but the young man was already running down the stairs.  "Please John, come back…" but he was already in the street, running away as fast as he possibly could.

In an instant, Albert was up and dressing himself.  "Great heavens, Walter, what do we do now?  Do we go to John's room and try to reason with him?"  He found the letter on the floor, which allowed him to at least partially deduce the reason for the young man's visit at so late an hour.

Walter held his head between his hands and thought for a few moments.  "We have been very good to John.  I don't think he will run directly to the magistrate.  Give him time to think tonight, and tomorrow, we can take him aside and discuss the matter."

"I most certainly hope you are correct, Walter," commented Albert while at the same time opening the letter that John had delivered.  Upon quickly glancing at the letter, he added, "And damn this news as well.  My father has died."

"Albert, my deepest condolences."  On some level, Walter was aware that this expression of sympathy was given in an unforgivably *'matter-of-fact'* tone.  His mind was filled with too many other concerns, and he failed to appreciate his friend's loss in the manner that he should have.

Albert paused, deep in thought for a moment, then said, "In truth, Walter, my father and I have scarcely communicated in twenty years, and I have not seen him for the last three.  Yet, the news is a blow.  Nevertheless, we do have more pressing concerns at this moment."

Walter ran his hands down his friend's arms.  "I am sure that John will not betray us."  After some further discussion, consoling and dressing, Walter returned home.


It might be thought strange that nights with little sleep can produce so many dreams.  The dreams experienced by both gentlemen that night were vivid, but they were brief and lacked complexity.  They were of gloomy and macabre possible outcomes of John's discovery.  Neither of the gentlemen kept his dream log in the morning and neither remembered any details of the night's confused visions.

As the sun rose, Mrs. Hewitt prepared breakfast, as she did six days per week.  As the last bite was being consumed, John was at the front of the shop, removing the shutters from the shop windows as was his duty.  Samuel assisted him.  Walter went down the stairs.  Albert had already arrived.

The shutters removed, the shop owner asked Samuel to go upstairs and see if Mrs. Hewitt needed any help.  He then relocked the door, delaying the opening of the shop.  Both men invited John into the private office at the rear of the store.  This was the very room where, some months earlier, negotiations with the Duke of Marlborough had been concluded.  It was a room that, in the past, John had glimpsed only briefly when collecting or delivering his employer's correspondence.  On this occasion, he was invited to sit in a chair opposite the owner's desk.

Walter began. "John, you learned a fact last night that we tried to conceal from you, and from everyone around us. We are not ashamed, but we are aware that the society in which we live does not approve of the nature of people such as us."

Albert Medhurst continued, "John, you know that Mr. Boniface is the kindest gentlemen that could ever be imagined. He has seen to it that you have had lodgings and employment, even after you committed a crime against him. He invites you nightly to his personal table for dinner. And, if I might say, I have also been very fond of you. I am sorry to say that we now need something from you."

Walter continued, "You found out last night that Mr. Medhurst and I are of a nature whereby we are attracted to men, specifically to each other, in the manner that other men might be attracted to women. For what you saw, the law would deem us guilty of a crime that they call sodomy. It is punishable by death. You were not meant to know of this, but through unfortunate circumstances, you now know. We are now forced to ask that you keep this information most secret. You know us, and you know that we are good and kind people. We care deeply for you, and for young Samuel. Our futures depend upon you telling no one of what you have seen, and, in a sense, your future and Samuel's depend upon this as well. If we can no longer operate our business, you and Samuel will no longer be employed."

John's eyes darted between them. He was obviously in a great quandary. He was familiar with the concept of sodomy. He was very much aware of the revulsion of society toward this offence and with the punishment that the law prescribed for those who committed it. He had recently been reminded of the importance of respecting and fearing the laws of the Kingdom. Even more recently, he had been instructed to respect and fear the laws of God and was aware of the Church of England's views toward this act as well. Now, he was being asked to turn his back upon both, and to protect men who were regarded by the law as criminals, and by the church as sinners. Yet, these two men, especially Mr. Boniface, had been immeasurably kind to him and to young

Samuel.  How could he betray them?  Finally, after much thought, he said, hesitatingly, "You have been very good to me indeed, Mr. Boniface, and you too Mr. Medhurst.  I will keep this secret.  Yes, Sirs, I will keep it to my grave."  John was sincere in his promise, but also heavily conflicted.

"We are so sorry to place this burden upon you, John."  Albert reached out his hand toward John's shoulder, but he shied away.

John predicted the next question and answered it before it was asked; "I didn't tell Samuel."

A moment was passed in silence so that all might compose their thoughts.  Once emotions seemed somewhat equalized, Walter gently asked, "Are we all in a fit state to start the day's business?"  Head nods, not words, answered in the affirmative.  The men went back to the shop and unlocked the door.


As the day progressed, John truly believed that the worst of the turmoil that his newfound knowledge had stirred was behind him.  It would not be correct to say that he no longer felt conflicted, but he had made a promise to keep a secret and he thought that this would be the end of the matter.  He was newly aware of something that he wished he had never found out, but surely there were more important things in the world than an instance of love between two men.

It seemed rather silly to John that he was even bothered by the matter, yet he undeniably was.  This expression of mutual affection was something done at night, in private, just as were similar acts between men and women.  Why should he care about such things?  Why did his newfound knowledge cause him such discomfort?  He didn't want to be troubled by what he knew, yet he was aware of the extreme enmity of society toward the act that these two gentlemen had committed.  As a life-long member of the society that harboured such enmity, he had naturally been imbued with the same intolerance. It would take some time to purge this emotion.


Walter and Albert did everything in their power to ensure that the day proceeded as normally as possible. Customers came and went, and the shop made a modest profit on the day. Dinner was served, consisting of a delicious lamb stew. Afterwards, John and Samuel returned to Shelton Street where they continued their reading lessons. Mrs. Hewitt went out to visit with a friend a couple of streets over, and Walter and Albert retired to the parlour for a more sombre than normal conversation.

"Albert," began Walter, "Last night, I was somewhat less than appropriately sympathetic when you told me of your father's passing. All the emotions and shocks of that moment combined, and I fear that I reacted unkindly. I am sorry for that, and I am also very deeply sorry for your loss."

Albert Medhurst was not quite sure how to respond. He shook his head, he forced an insincere smile, then he said, "I thank you, Walter. And I took no offense last night. It was indeed a moment of extreme emotion, and I must admit that I scarcely remember how you reacted as I was so upset about all that was happening. There was both this news and John's unexpected arrival occurring at the same time; I think neither of us were in an entirely disciplined mental state. Anyway, the mass for my father is to be tomorrow afternoon. If I may absent myself from the shop for a short time..."

"Of course, Albert. Take all the time you need. Would you like the full day to discharge your family duties?"

"No," responded Albert, almost aggressively. "Thank you, but as I mentioned, my father and I have not been on good terms ever since I was a boy. I have only rarely seen him in the last two decades. Yet, I feel that I should make a showing at the funeral mass." Albert's family worshiped in a small brick building at Soho Square, one of the few Roman Catholic churches in the London area.  As a Roman Catholic, Albert was denied several privileges under English law.  For example, he could not sit in parliament as a member of the House of Commons.  Fortunately, he had little desire to pursue such an office.  After a brief pause and a sip of gin, Albert continued, "Did you notice any issues with John today, following our discussion this morning?"

"He was troubled, even at dinner." replied Walter.  "He lacked some of the carefree attitude that, usually, he positively exudes."

"Damn it, Walter.  If only he hadn't opened that door."

Walter nodded, then said, "He had forgotten to give you your letter.  He was following his sense of duty by running it to you as soon as he realized.  If only we had been a bit more attentive for someone knocking.  Now, I fear that John is a victim of what he knows.  We have no choice but to require him to keep the secret, but it is a great burden that we place on him."

Albert suggested, "We will have to be very good to him, going forward."

"That was always my intention.  Let's face it my friend, I am not going to live forever, and there is a gray hair or two showing on your forehead.  Given both of our natures, neither of us are at all likely to ever have children to continue our business.  You, of course, are the primary inheritor of the shop but I think I could envision a time, far in the future of course, when it belonged to John, and perhaps Samuel as well.  As I grow old, I would prefer to know this to be its fate rather than expecting it to be sold off to the highest bidder or closed up altogether."

"I would like to see that too.  Gray hair indeed!  Well, maybe one or two."  The quantity of gray hairs on Albert's head could not possibly be determined in the pale candlelight.  Two more glasses of gin poured, he continued, "And in the shorter term, can we continue to tend our own fires in my room from time to time, or does this now present too much risk?"

Walter said plainly, "John knows.  Nothing else has changed.  I honestly believe that he will keep our secret to his grave, as he promised to do.  Nothing needs to change between us."  In a softer tone, he continued, "I think, in the near future, you should visit the ironmonger to purchase a sliding bolt for your door."

## Chapter 12 – Pea-Soup and Nerves

Throughout that cold and wet spring, five people worked in a small, somewhat old building in Westminster. Four spent their days downstairs in the shop while the fifth laboured above. There were gnawing secrets, and these suffocated some of the joy that used to permeate that place, but there were still lighthearted moments. Furthermore, dinner was always delicious and lovingly prepared.

One morning during these weeks, John and Samuel had awoken and dressed in their room in Shelton Street. The older boy looked out through the room's almost opaque window and noted that he was able to see even less than usual. "It's a pea-souper out there," he called out to Samuel, referring to London's notorious fog.

The boys didn't fully comprehend how dense the fog was until they stepped out onto the street. Shelton street was socked in with a dense, acrid blanket made up of both water vapour and coal smoke. It was fortunate that they knew their way as a pedestrian less familiar with the streets would have found it quite impossible to navigate. A carriage driver was observed leading his horses from in front and citizens felt their way along walls for fear of losing their direction. The great city was strangely silent with all movement having ground to a crawl.

By the time the pair arrived at the bookshop, Samuel was wheezing and coughing from the toxic air. John let him inside to catch his breath, then proceeded to remove the shutters by himself. Mr. Medhurst arrived in time to assist in the final phase of this task. When these two entered the shop, Mr. Boniface was already ushering Samuel upstairs to the ministrations of his housekeeper. She provided a cup of tea to wash down a bit of bread and jam, and the boy was back at his duties within half an hour.

As Samuel swept, Mr. Medhurst commented, "I think we are unlikely to welcome any customers before this fog clears." Throughout the morning, his prediction proved correct. One man was seen briefly at the door, but he was simply feeling his way along the front of the shop as he navigated blindly through the impenetrable haze. Not a single customer entered the store.

By early afternoon, it was possible to walk without the imminent fear of bumping into something or someone, yet driving a carriage or cart would still have been quite treacherous. The atmosphere had penetrated the shop and young Samuel was finding it difficult to breathe once again. As such, it was quite to the surprise of all when one of Mr. Boniface's most favoured customers stepped through the door. "Good afternoon, my good man," Mr. Boniface said to him. "In what way may we assist you?"

"Good day, Sir," replied the man. "I do have business, but please forgive me. I have travelled far through this infernal fog. I must catch my breath." His voice was hoarse, and he let out a worrying cough.

"Of course. John, please fetch a cup of water for this man."

The water consumed and his eyes wiped with the corner of his handkerchief, the man was able to discharge his duties. "I thank you kindly, Sir. I serve His Lordship the Duke of Hamilton. His Lordship has instructed me to seek you out and to advise you that he has, in his London residence, some many volumes, the property of his late father, and he craves your experienced eye to look over these and offer any such sums as you may feel correct for their purchase." He handed Mr. Boniface what appeared to be a single sheet of paper, saying, "This is but a partial listing of the contents of the lot on offer, Sir."

Walter Boniface looked intrigued, but not excited. "I think that there may be some moderate value in these items. In what location, and at what date might I be able to view the books?"

"My master is available this very afternoon, Sir, if it is convenient for you, and I do have a dogcart by which I might convey you hence."

Walter Boniface looked toward the shop door.  The fog had thinned just to the point where he could see a horse and a small vehicle in the street.  Given that there had been no other business conducted in the shop that day, he considered that this was the most appropriate moment possible for him to absent himself.  He said to the man, "This very moment is convenient indeed.  I shall come with you presently."  After speaking briefly to Mr. Medhurst and ensuring that he might be able to serve the throngs of customers who were absent on that day, Walter donned his coat and hat and left with the servant.

From John's point of view, working in the shop with Mr. Medhurst in charge felt slightly more awkward than when the owner was present. That gentleman had always been kind to him, but unlike Mr. Boniface, he was not to be thanked for saving his very life.  Additionally, Mr. Medhurst was a Roman Catholic, this being in a period when John was, for the first time, studying the tenets and beliefs endemic to the Church of England.  It was not a matter of dislike for the man in any way, but simply a lack of similar views that fueled this tension.

Mr. Medhurst also found the afternoon a bit awkward.  Like his friend, he also trusted John, but perhaps not with the same level of certainty. As a result, even though the afternoon passed with the older and the younger employee each treating the other cordially, the level of tension rose, nonetheless.

Had the society around him, and his newfound faith, not placed such pressures upon John, he would have been entirely at ease with the love that Messrs. Boniface and Medhurst felt for one another.  To his mind, there was no reason that this affection, or the act of its expression, should be deemed so wicked or sinful.  He had on many occasions asked himself if society might be wrong in its condemnation of men such as these.  Unfortunately, every time he pondered this question, he remembered his station in life.  He was little more than a boy, and one who had recently been confined in prison for a criminal act.  Who was he to question the long-established values of both society and the church, as well as the laws of the Kingdom?  He concluded that the two gentlemen must have committed a terrible wrong because everyone around him asserted that such an act was a terrible wrong.  The reason behind this nearly universal condemnation must simply be outside of his understanding.


Eventually, the clock advanced to the closing hour, but Mr. Boniface had not yet returned.  The shutters were put up, all save for the one over the shop door and the trio waited therein for his return.  Mrs. Hewitt came downstairs to inquire as to the nature of the delay and was advised that they awaited the return of the shop owner.  "Well, I shall keep dinner warm to the best of my ability," she said in a slightly annoyed tone as she returned to the first-floor kitchen.

More than half an hour after the shutters went up, Mr. Boniface returned at last.  He was emptyhanded and looking uncharacteristically annoyed.  "I have just expended the afternoon in the company of a Scottish lord trying to peddle a pile of second-rate books as if they were the Crown Jewels!  I then couldn't find a cab in this accursed fog and have had to walk all the way from Portman Square.  I trust dinner is ready.  Well, let's go then."  He led the party up the stairs.

Dinner passed with scarcely a word.  As it ended, Mrs. Hewitt filled up Mr. Boniface's teacup.  He took a sip and spurted out, "Confound it woman!  Cold as ice!  Can you not make a hot cup of tea?"

Mrs. Hewitt dutifully produced some fresh, hot tea as John and Samuel bade their goodnights and headed out into the fog.  As they walked, Samuel said to John, "Mr. Boniface certainly seemed angry tonight, didn't he John?"

John smiled at the younger boy, saying, "I think he just had a bad day, wasting a lot of time with that Scottish lord that he told us of, yet being unable to buy any books.  The shop lost money today.  I'm sure all will be better tomorrow."  Neither boy was aware that Mr. Boniface was, at that very moment, in the parlour with Mrs. Hewitt, offering a sincere and humble apology for his unkind behaviour toward her.

Hurtful words to his housekeeper having been redeemed, Walter walked over to the room above the cobbler shop (to which Albert had returned some minutes earlier).  "Is all put right with Mrs. Hewitt?" Albert asked as his friend entered.

"I think it is," Walter answered.  "Damn, I don't know what made me snap at her like that."

"A frustrating afternoon, the fog, worry over our secret, and the fact that the shop had not a single sale on the whole day; you have a lot of things on your mind.  Sometimes anger meant for one is expressed toward another."  Albert poured two glasses of gin.

"The only person I'm angry at this day is that bothersome Scottish lord!" Walter was clearly still disquieted.  "Upset with me because I wouldn't pay him double, nay, triple, the value of some old moldy books stacked in a pile on the floor owing to the fact that his shelves, although designed for books, are now filled with artifacts plundered from the ancient ruins of Egypt.  He then dismissed me into this cursed fog without asking his man who drove me there in a poorly sprung dogcart to do me the courtesy of driving me back once again.  An afternoon wasted, and nothing to show for it."

Albert pointed at his friend's glass, then at his lips and simply said, "Walter, gin, now."  Never before had it been so needed.

"Oh, my dear Albert, I seem to have just proven you correct."  Walter took his friend's advice in regard to the gin.  "Just as I lashed out at Mrs.

Hewitt at dinner time, I have now done the same to you.  For the second time tonight, I must offer an apology."

Albert actually laughed slightly, an unexpected reaction.  "Well, I do like to be correct, and I understand.  Let's put Scottish lords out of our minds, shall we?  I have been waiting all day to read to you about last night's dreams."

"I trust that they in no way involve Scottish lords."

"Not at all."

"Then do proceed."

"Well then," Albert began, "you may have noticed when looking at maps of the Thames that one might imagine that river to be the body of a great serpent."

"I think that observation might be made of many rivers," Walter observed.

"Quite true, but being residents of this great city, we more often tend to turn our attention toward our own river.  At any rate, on the map that I was observing, this serpent suddenly came alive.  I watched as it slithered across the map of London and beyond.  I then found myself transported into the streets and in all those places where the serpent had crawled on the map was found only destruction; never a house or shop or even cathedral standing.  There was destruction as far as the eye could see.  Soon after, the serpent returned and it changed bodily into the very image of our deceased king, the late George III.  The King, appearing as he did in his more magnificent days, stood proudly over all this destruction.  In a matter which might interest you, Walter, I saw the bookshop standing unharmed although the remainder of the street and the entire city as far as I could see was obliterated utterly, reduced to smoking ruins."

"Well, that was quite a dark vision my friend," commented Walter. "The map from which the serpent originated, was it printed in a book in our inventory?"

"I do believe it was," confirmed Albert.

"So, the serpent was escaping from our shop, then causing this calamity. In regard to our late King, did you experience any feelings or emotions upon seeing his image?"

"Revulsion, one might even say hatred.  This is strange, as I never felt this way toward our late King; perhaps somewhat for the current one."

Walter thought for a moment before offering the proposal, "Perhaps the identity of the king is not important.  We often see people in dreams as youthful, even though they have since matured.  Similarly, even though George III is now dead and was unseen for some time before his death, it may be that his image simply represents those who have power over you.  It would take great power to destroy this city, and none have more power than The King, regardless of which king that may be."

"Yet the snake was destroying the city before it transformed into The King.  What is the relationship between a great snake and The King?" Albert was confused by his friend's analysis.

Walter asked, "Were you happy about the snake causing such destruction?"  Albert shook his head to indicate that he was not.  "Were you in control of that snake?"  Again, a shake of the head to indicate the negative.  "Well then, who was in control?"  Albert hesitated.  Walter offered some further coaching, "This was your dream, Albert, and if you held a belief within the dream, even if it was arrived at without evidence, then that belief is valid.  Who, by your belief, was controlling the serpent?"

Albert thought for a short moment, then said, "It was controlled by what The King represents.  I think that The King, in my dream, represents the collected opinions of our nation and society, and being defender of the faith, the opinions of the Church of England as well. Why would I feel that way?  The destruction of London is most certainly not what either king or society wants."

Walter pressed the question, "Setting that aside for a moment, what does the snake represent?"

Not less than a minute passed in silence after this question before it was answered.  Walter sat, patiently sipping gin, while his friend thought.  Finally, he said without great certainty, "The serpent is the weapon wielded by that society.  I felt that the snake's purpose was to destroy all that I, or we, hold dear, and I suppose that we hold this city dear."  After a further pause, he continued, "But it left the bookshop untouched.  How does that fact reconcile with my interpretation?"

"I take it that in your dream, you had no inkling as to why the bookshop was spared?"

"None at all," Albert responded.  "I did wonder in the dream why the serpent spared the shop but came up with no theory on the matter."

Walter thought for a while longer, then asked his friend, "You felt that the snake was the weapon wielded by society.  Was that weapon wielded against us?  Against our love?"

Albert could neither confirm nor deny this tentative interpretation, but its suggestion caused a connection to be made in his mind.  It was a connection that seemed akin to those experienced when asleep.  It seemed every bit as ephemeral as a dream.  In an effort to capture the fleeting thought before it faded forever, Albert quickly blurted it out to his friend: "The bookshop is our castle.  Within its ramparts is where we make our stand against the attacks of the world; against their hatred of our nature.  The castle was held; the snake did not breach it..."  Immediately after these unfiltered thoughts had been blurted out, the more disciplined portions of Alberts mind once again asserted their control.  Only moments later, feeling a bit embarrassed by his unmoderated utterance, he explained, "I say, Walter, I cannot imagine where those words came from.  They seemed profound as I said them, but they seem so very silly just seconds later."

Walter smiled.  "Albert," he said kindly, "Your words were not silly.  They were examples of raw and unconsidered honesty.  I think that I have just been introduced to a little part of your mind that you have never before shared with any being upon this Earth.  For just one moment, you touched your dreams while your body was yet awake, and you shared one of those dreams with me at the very moment that it was happening.  Even our dream logs cannot record our visions with that level of intimacy, and I am honoured to have shared with you this most personal moment.  You have redeemed my bad day.  Thank you, my very dear friend."

The couple tended their own fires long into the evening.  It would be significantly later than usual before Walter returned to his rooms above the bookshop.

## Chapter 13 – The Laws of God and Men

The days and weeks passed.  The cold drear of early spring progressed into the showiness of May.  Flowers adorned the city's squares and parks, their sweet perfume entirely undetectable amidst the stench of horse and humanity.  The incessant din of hooves and iron-rimmed wheels on the cobbled streets, the shouting of hawkers and a thousand other obnoxious noises more than silenced the songs of the birds.  The glass windows of the bookshop shut out the major fraction of the disagreeable scents and sounds, but not all of them.  Some days, the stench and the noise made the shop seem not unlike the tenements of the dirtiest and most drunken alleyways of London.  Yet, all did their duty.

John continued to be tortured by his knowledge of the relationship between the two booksellers.  He desperately wanted to accept their nature, but the contemptuous views of the society to which he belonged made this impossible for him.  Within his mind, the conflict roiled to the point where he decided that he needed to discuss the matter with someone; but who could he trust?  Who would not be instantaneously judgemental, and who could offer wise and salient advice?  The answer to these questions seemed clear.  John would speak to someone of the highest moral standards, one who he believed to be endowed with great wisdom, and with great empathy.  He would speak to a highly respected member of clergy.

It was on a Friday, following dinner over the bookshop, that John finally mustered the courage to discuss his conflicted mind with the Reverend Mr. Hillyard.  He sought only advice, and he thought that this venerated man of God would be highly skilled at dispensing this commodity.  Who else but a preacher could offer him solace in the throes of his inner turmoil?  He had held onto his secret for too long.  If he did not relieve the pressure that he felt inside, he would burst.  He had no choice but to discuss his situation with someone, and he was certain that the Reverend Mr. Hillyard would be best qualified to assist him in his confusion.

That evening as the boys walked down the stairs from the first floor of the bookshop, the hour was growing late.  Even so, the lengthening days of approaching summer offered an enduring flourish of orange sunshine.  "Go back to the room, Samuel," John advised his younger companion as they walked toward Shelton Street.  "I shall be there presently.  I need to speak with someone."  With that, he walked to the church where he spent his Sunday mornings.  Sheepishly, he went up to the door and stepped inside.

The Reverend Mr. Hillyard was in a small room at the rear of the church.  Hearing the door close, he stepped out.  "Of what service might I be, young man?"

John stammered, "Sir, Mr. Reverend, might... may I ask a question?"

The pastor motioned for him to come closer, then said, "If you are troubled or are in need of spiritual guidance, then I shall endeavour to provide you with an answer to your question, or at the very least, to assist you in finding the means to answer it for yourself."  It was at this moment that the pastor recognised John as one of the boys that Mrs. Hewitt had recently been bringing to services on Sundays.

"Sir, Reverend..., if I were to know of someone who has committed a crime, a sin against God, yet that person has been very good to me and to others, and is a very good person all in all..."  John's voice trailed off as his nerve faltered.

The preacher asked, "What is the nature of this crime and sin?"  He quickly observed that John was reluctant to reply so he did not press the matter.

John had intended to reveal the specific nature of the matter so that the trusted preacher might be able to offer the most appropriate advice, but at that moment, he thought better of his intent.  After a pause, he found the words to continue, "If I knew such a person, a good person, am I required to tell of their offence?"

The Reverend Mr. Hillyard offered the advice, "If this person is of a general goodness, then he most certainly does not want to live with a sin on his conscience.  He must answer to the courts of men for the crime, and he must accept the mercy of Our Lord, who, if asked, will grant forgiveness of the sin."

John looked with grave seriousness at the Reverend Mr. Hillyard.  "Must I tell the authorities of his crime?"

The preacher dearly wanted to know the nature of the crime being discussed, but he was sensitive enough to John's emotional state that he didn't insist upon an answer to his earlier question.  He asked, "Has this man made peace with Our Lord for his sin and is he now repentant, or does he attempt to hide his sin from God?  Does he persist in the commission of his sin, and his crime?"

John remembered that Mr. Boniface had told him that he and Mr. Medhurst were not ashamed for what they were doing on that night when he had inadvertently intruded upon them, so he was confident in answering, "I am quite certain that the sin is still being committed."

The reverend raised his eyebrows, then offered the advice, "It may be possible to hide a crime from men, but you cannot hide a sin from God.  My boy, to bring an unremorseful criminal to justice also grants that criminal the motivation to repent his sins.  In this way, following any appropriate punishment on Earth, he may be welcomed into paradise thereafter.  Therefore, to report such a crime is not only a requirement, but it is also a great act of kindness to the one who has committed the crime.  And might I add, my young friend, that if you conceal a criminal, then you too are attempting to hide that person's sins from God.  You will be equally unsuccessful, and your own soul may be in peril for the effort."

John thanked the preacher and departed.  He had much to think about. He desperately wanted to be a good person in his own right.  Every fibre of his being wanted to do what was right and just, but he was so very deeply conflicted as to what that might be.

John was a young man, an orphan who had, only by the grace of God, avoided the workhouse.  But was that good fortune actually by the grace of God, or was it by the grace of Mr. Boniface?  He recalled some six years earlier being a poor, destitute young boy, recently orphaned and hungry.  Mr. Boniface had hired him to sweep out the bookshop and run errands, much as he had more recently done for Samuel.  And it was Mr. Boniface who had forgiven him after his betrayal, and it was Mr. Boniface who had paid the rent on his room while he was in prison. It was Mr. Boniface who invited him to dine at his table six nights per week.  Never had a young man greater cause to be thankful to a bene-factor than he.

Weighing against all of this were the words of the Reverend Mr. Hillyard.  *'It is not only a requirement to report a crime, but also a great act of kindness to the criminal.'*  If either Mr. Boniface or Mr. Medhurst was to meet his maker with so great a sin on his head, would his soul not be eternally damned?

John then, once again, heard that other voice in his head, the one whose source he could not identify.  It was not the church speaking, nor was it the law.  It was not even the collective voice of the society that surrounded him.  Where did this recurring question come from?  John asked himself, one more time, 'Could the church, the law, and indeed the views of an entire society, be entirely wrong?  If two people truly love one another, regardless of their sex, why is it a sin, a crime and an abhorrence for them to express that love?'  This thought lingered for some time in his head, but as before, he found it impossible to process. One young man could not dismiss a symphony heard from all quarters that universally denounced the act undertaken by Messrs. Boniface and Medhurst.  John dismissed this thought, for the last time.

The next morning, a Saturday, John and Samuel reported for duty at the shop.  Samuel would have described it as an uneventful day.  For John, however, the whole day was a strained effort to act normally while ignoring something so big, so obvious, that it filled his every thought.  It was as if there were something gigantic and unmissable in the bookshop, such as an elephant, yet he was forced to pretend that it was not there.  Messrs. Boniface and Medhurst were unaware of the level of turmoil churning inside their young employee.  They believed that John had made peace with his decision to remain silent about their nature, even though they could not avoid a degree of underlying concern in the matter.

When business ended for the day, the shop owner and staff went upstairs for the evening meal.  This passed cordially, yet less joyfully than normal, much to the consternation of young Samuel.  Saturday was the day that Mrs. Hewitt outdid herself with her preparations.  She had roasted a duck this week, and there were delicious vegetables and fresh bread on the side.  There was cake as well, sweet and delicious.  Samuel found it impossible to understand why there was far less conversation and general familial joy than usual.  Mrs. Hewitt found this a bit discomforting as well.

Saturday evening ended and on the Sunday that followed, John and Samuel attended services at the church in the company of Mrs. Hewitt. Following the services, the pair went their own way while Mrs. Hewitt remained at the church to undertake some volunteer work.  A short time later, the Reverend Mr. Hillyard had completed his ecclesiastical duties, for the moment at least.  Confirming that Mrs. Hewitt was still on the premises, he sent for her and requested that she join him in a small room at the rear of the church.  When she arrived, he invited her to sit, and he explained the reason for the requested audience.  "Two days ago," he explained, "the older of the two youths who you accompany to church services each Sunday came to visit me.  He asked me questions about the morality of reporting a crime to authorities, and whether he was obliged to make such a report if he felt the perpetrator to be a good person overall.  He seemed troubled, as if he were aware of some crime of a serious nature.  I could not learn from him any further details about the crime in question.  I hoped that you may be able to shed some light upon this mystery so that we may offer more informed and inspired advice to the young man."

Mrs. Hewitt outwardly kept her calm.  "I am sorry, I'm sure that I cannot."  She said nothing more.

Leaving the church, Mrs. Hewitt walked through the neighbourhood for some time.  She then went to Shelton Street, the rather run-down and muddy lane populated with many disagreeable and dangerous-looking people.  She searched for the place where John and Samuel kept their room.  She knew the address to be sought out thanks to some prior conversations with John, but she had never before been there.  Consequently, some minutes were passed in finding the location.  Knocking at the door of their room, she found that the boys were not at home, so she retired to a safer neighbourhood and returned later.  When she knocked at the door for the second time, John answered.  He was astonished to see his employer's housekeeper.  "Goodness, Mrs. Hewitt, I would not have expected you to be here.  How can I be of assistance?"

"Can we speak alone, John?"  He asked Samuel to go outside.  Once the younger boy had departed, Mrs. Hewitt continued, "The Reverend Mr. Hillyard tells me that you spoke to him on Friday last."

"Ay," replied John, "I did at that."

"He suggested that you might be aware of a crime, and that you had sought his advice as to the morality and necessity of reporting it."  John just nodded his head to confirm that her statement was correct.  "Does this crime involve Mr. Boniface?"  John nodded his head again.  "Does it also involve Mr. Medhurst?"

"My word, Mrs. Hewitt," John said with further astonishment, "you know about them."

"I have known for years, John. I have been respectful enough to two kind and generous gentlemen to say nothing about it. How is it that you became aware?" John related an abridged and undetailed version of his discovery over the cobbler shop. Having heard this, Mrs. Hewitt continued, "Now that you are aware, you must show the same respect that I have shown. No more words of this matter John, not to anyone. You have Mr. Boniface to thank for your very life and you cannot be such a fool as to fail to recognize this fact."

"But the Reverend said that a crime must be reported, and that their souls are in peril if they are not brought to justice."

For the first time since John had known her, Mrs. Hewitt became angry. "What crime?" she asked in a muffled yell. "The Reverend likely thought you to be speaking of a theft or robbery in which someone has been deprived of property, or perhaps a murder where they have been deprived of life. Who is deprived of what in this matter? There has been no loss suffered by anyone. I implore you John, hold your tongue." With that, she marched out of the room.

Young Samuel saw Mrs. Hewitt leaving the building, but in her distraught state, she didn't notice him. He went back to the room to ask John what had transpired, but John refused to tell him. He then asked, "Why have there been so many secrets as of late?"

John just looked at him and said, "Be thankful for those secrets." That evening, the two used the battered old bible to help Samuel to improve his reading. All the time, John was hoping to find some passage that might calm his inner turmoil. Instead, they read about a man who was caught picking up sticks on the sabbath and brought before Moses for punishment. By the explicit command of God, that man was stoned to death. The law is the law.

As John tried (with little success) to sleep that night, he found the flaw in Mrs. Hewitt's argument.  He asked himself if the advice of the Reverend Mr. Hillyard would have been different if the pastor had known the nature of the crime.  Based upon all that John understood about the views of the church, and about broader society (of which churchmen are prominent figures), he was quite certain that had the preacher known the crime in question to be sodomy, he would have been even more insistent that it be reported.  The Reverend would have likely contacted authorities himself and arranged for the information to be forced from John's lips if he would not offer it freely.  Indeed, he decided, it was a good thing for him to refuse to tell the Reverend the nature of the crime.

In the very brief time that John did sleep that night, he had dreams that might have rivaled Mr. Boniface's in complexity.  He saw himself standing at the gates of heaven but being denied entry for the sin of not reporting the supposedly heinous crime of which he was aware.  Next, he was facing Mr. Boniface and Mr. Medhurst, both of them demanding to know why he had betrayed them as they were stoned to death.  He was aware that executions in England were usually carried out by hanging and never by stoning, but thanks to the evening's bible-reading session, God's preferred method was fresh in his mind.  He dreamt of Mrs. Hewitt running at him in anger, her face becoming that of a grizzled old witch as she approached.  He dreamt of the bookshop in flames, and he seemed to believe that he had lit the fire.  He saw many more images, dark and frightening.

When he woke very early in the morning with a start, the light of the sun was just beginning to seep through the filthy windowpane.  He had come to a decision.  His soul might be damned.  The souls of Mr. Boniface and Mr. Medhurst, and even Mrs. Hewitt might be damned, but he resolved that he would say nothing.  Even though every element of society told him that he must speak out, and even his own conscience told him that he should do so, he would choose to ignore them all.  He would remain silent, and he would mend his relationship with Mr.

Boniface and Mr. Medhurst.  As far as John was concerned at that moment, the matter was resolved.

This resolution was merely an illusion.  The maintenance of that illusion would consume all of John's personal willpower for many days to come.

# Chapter 14 – Society's Error

Several weeks had passed since John had made his untimely entry into Mr. Medhurst's room.  For knowing the secret, there was less joy in his days.  He still completed all the requirements of his employment.  He sold books, he ran errands, he loaned Samuel the key to Mr. Medhurst's room so that the boy might clean and organize it once or twice per week.  He continued to take the evening meal at the wooden table in the kitchen above the bookshop and later each evening, he continued teaching Samuel to read using the torn and tattered old bible.

John also took to walking, alone, late in the night.  He would walk past the shuttered bookshop and along the street upon which it stood.  On some of these nights, there was a light in the window of Mr. Boniface's parlour above the shop.  On other nights, smoke came from a specific chimney pot over the cobbler shop, which the young man had determined to be the outlet of Mr. Medhurst's fireplace.  Never were both signs observed on the same night.  He therefore concluded that what he had witnessed while delivering the letter was not a unique event, but rather a frequent occurrence.

Sometimes, John would hide in a narrow alley between nearby shops.  It mattered little whether the parlour light was lit, or the chimney pot had smoke, for in either case one of the two gentlemen would be seen walking along the street some time after the hour of ten, but before midnight.  Never was there an exception.  John determined that in one location or the other, Mr. Boniface and Mr. Medhurst were indeed spending every evening together.

The days that followed these nighttime escapades unfolded just as had the days before.  Walter, Albert and John all sold books and earned commissions, more on some days, fewer on others.  All outwardly seemed normal, mundane, unchanging.  However, on one particular

Saturday in mid June, there was a minor change from the ordinary routine.

It was a moment of only the slightest unpleasantness, a minor barrage of critical words, a small rebuke from an employer to an employee.  Mr. Boniface observed John handling a valuable book with less care than it might have deserved, or at least that was his perception.  He raised his voice slightly to John, ordering him to be more careful.  He may have been wrong in accusing the young man, for John did not believe that he had handled the book incautiously.  He may also have been justified.  At any rate, the mishandling of the book was the smallest of offences, regardless of whether it had actually occurred, or not.  Mr. Boniface, his rebuke being registered, quickly forgot the matter and pressed on with the labours at hand.

In John's mind, the slightly angry words made the shop, and his relationship with its owner, seem just a little bit colder still.  The bookshop had long been John's place of employment, but it also was a most welcoming place, a place where he felt safe from the unkind streets of London.  The small rebuke made it feel decidedly less welcoming, and less safe.  Thoughts of his employer's moment of trivial anger soured the rest of the workday, and the evening meal.

It was not so much the rebuke itself that induced these feelings in John.  While not a frequent occurrence, he had occasionally received some small oral correction from Mr. Boniface in the past and these had never deeply troubled him before.  For some unknown reason, this time it did.  The incident, (if it was severe enough to be called that), acted as a further complication of the extremely complex relationship that the two now shared.  There were too many secrets in that bookshop, or perhaps one too few.  John knew something that he wished he didn't.  He also knew that Mrs. Hewitt was aware of the secret, but that she did not revel her knowledge to the gentlemen.  Did those gentlemen know that she knew, yet pretend otherwise?  It was all too complicated for his mind to process.  This minor bit of friction between himself and Mr. Boniface just marginally raised that level of complication.

John also felt compelled to protect young Samuel who knew nothing about any of this.  He envied the young boy's ignorance.

Following dinner as the confused young man walked back to Shelton Street, he felt even more deeply troubled than he had for the last several weeks.  How could he justify his silence?  He was convinced that God wanted him to tell someone every detail of what he knew.  Sadly, he faced the difficulty that every person he might possibly speak to would be hopelessly biased against the two gentlemen, or in the case of Mrs. Hewitt, hopelessly biased in favour of them.  The two strong opinions were equally unhelpful at that juncture.  If only there were someone who would be unbiased and confidential, who would hear his concerns and give balanced advice.  Perhaps someone else of the same nature as Mr. Boniface and Mr. Medhurst?  No.  John would have no idea where to find such a person.  Furthermore, that individual would hardly be unbiased in his own right.  There was simply no one with whom to speak.

And what of his own soul?  Shelton Street could be a dangerous part of town.  There were robbers in that neighbourhood who would stick a knife in a man's heart for the couple of shillings in his pocket.  What if he met his end with this terrible secret on his conscience?  He passed yet another night in a turmoil of nightmares and visions of hellfire.

The next morning being a Sunday, John and Samuel attended the services at the little church.  They listened to an impassioned sermon powerfully delivered by the Reverend Mr. Hillyard.  The old pastor truly was a great orator.  He had an ability to inspire the minds of his flock while truly saying very little of substance.  Such an ability was surely endemic to his vocation, yet this individual raised the talent to its zenith.  He simply presented motes of advice, some self-evident and some borrowed from scripture, and he delivered these to his enraptured audience with unwavering conviction and no small measure of eloquence.  In this pursuit, none could deny his skill

One proclamation from the rather lengthy sermon resonated deeply with John, all the more so in his current, severely conflicted, state.  The Reverend Mr. Hillyard preached,

> *"Embrace the sinner who repents his sins.  Embrace also the sinner who knows not that he has sinned so that you may show him his sins and show him also the way that he might become repentant.  But of the sinner who knows that he sins, and yet says that in his sins he feels neither shame nor guilt, embrace that sinner not, for that sinner has denied the mercy of Our Saviour.  Instead, bring that sinner to justice, as hard as such justice might be.  Only in this way may the unrepentant sinner come to hear the word of Our Saviour.  By this path, he may yet gain salvation but if he continues to deny Our Saviour, even in his heart, he shall be denied paradise when his time in this world has ended."*

Following the service, John parted ways with Samuel, sending the younger boy back to Shelton Street alone.  He then walked.  He walked further from home than he had ever been before.  He walked to London Bridge, then to the south side of the Thames and amongst the warehouses and factories of Southwark.  He made his way through unfamiliar streets and dangerous alleys until he came upon Westminster Bridge.  Crossing this bridge, he walked past Westminster Abbey, that great edifice where kings took their crown and where all manner of royalty and nobility was laid to rest.  Passing palaces and grand houses at the closest respectable distance, it was growing dark before he finally returned to his room in Shelton Street.  He had intended to walk as a means of helping himself to think, but in truth, he found himself walking to avoid thinking.

"John, I was so worried about you," Samuel blurted as he came through the door.

"I'm sorry to worry you, Samuel. I had things that I needed to do." He didn't say anything more.

When nighttime came, John's state was such that there was no use in him even trying to sleep. A fugue was playing itself out within his mind. According to the sermon given by Reverend Mr. Hillyard, at least as he had interpreted it, God wanted him to betray the two men to whom he owed everything. The King's law and English society wanted the same. But Mrs. Hewitt, the kindest spokesperson for the church, and for all of England, beseeched him to hold his tongue. And his own conscience told him that he had Mr. Boniface to thank for his life and livelihood. John also felt great responsibility for young Samuel who had been saved from a terrible fate by the intervention of Mr. Boniface and who would once again face that fate if his employer were denounced. And was the crime of Messrs. Boniface and Medhurst so horrible as all said that it was? Oh, it was too much! John tossed and turned into the night, entirely unable to process the questions that flooded into his head.

Eventually, John made a fateful decision; one that would change many lives, and none for the better. Despite the lateness of the hour, he told Samuel that he needed to go out for another walk. He went out in the night and straight to the nearest police office. There, he spoke to a constable by the name of Jenkins. A more senior officer was called over who was known as Saunders. Finally, the magistrate was sent for, that being one Lord Stephenson. John Kenworthy told all that he knew, and his world came crashing down.

From the moment of his disclosure, John was reduced to an automaton. It was as if he were one of those clockwork contraptions that wealthy nobles would wind up and set upon their tables. These contraptions would move about to the wonderment of all but were capable of nothing more than their gears and springs commanded them to do. John held nothing back, nor, in his state, could he have willed himself to do so. He told the constables of his delivery of the letter to Mr. Medhurst, of the unheard knocks at the door, and of what he had seen when he opened the door.  He told them of the gentlemen's ardent request that he hold his tongue and of the signs that he had figured out to indicate whether they were spending the evening above the bookshop, or above the cobbler shop.  He told them that the Reverend Mr. Hillyard's sermons had made him aware of the authority of God and how he had wrestled with his conscience.  He also did not fail to tell them of the kindness that the two gentlemen had shown to him and young Samuel.

The constables and the magistrate then asked John some very strange questions.  "Did you observe which man committed the assault, and which willingly received it?"  John was unaware that there had been an assault, but he did describe to his inquisitors the positions of each man at the first moment he saw them.  "Was there emission?"  That question required some sheepish explanation from the constable, but John was certain that he did not know.  "Was either of the gentlemen dressed in women's clothes?"  No, he had already said that they wore no clothes at all.  "Were any other mollies seen either on the premises or in the area?"  No, none that he recognized.  "Were there any dogs or other animals present."  No.  "Have you ever witnessed either gentleman visiting a house, possibly one that looks like a small inn that is frequented by many men or boys?"  He had not.  Finally, "Have you made attempts to extort either money or favour from either of the individuals through threats of exposing them?"  Most certainly not!

Constable Saunders hired a hackney coach.  He and John rode from the police office through the dark nighttime streets and finally along the street in front of the bookshop.  John pointed out all localities of interest including Mr. Boniface's parlour window and Mr. Medhurst's chimney pot.  They surveyed the locations of side alleys and hiding points from which they may watch the street on the next night.

Saunders requested that John meet him at a nearby locksmith shop very early in the morning so that he may have duplicates made of the keys to Mr. Medhurst's room, in case they may be needed.  He also instructed John to pursue his employment and all other aspects of his relationship with the two gentlemen as if nothing was abnormal, then, following dinner the next day, to report to a location a short distance from the shop to meet with the constables.  The cab driver dropped John off in Shelton Street before returning the constable to the police office.

It was on the order of three o'clock in the morning when John returned to his room.  He slipped in quietly so as not to wake Samuel.  He crawled into his bed, but he did not sleep.  He wept instead.

Far from bringing the spiritual relief that he though it should, John's denouncement sent him into a spiral of guilt.  He had just catastrophically betrayed Walter Boniface and Albert Medhurst, the only two men who had ever been kind to him.  He had also betrayed Mrs. Hewitt, the only woman who had shown him kindness since the day that his mother had succumbed to fever when he was only a young child.  And he had betrayed Samuel, the boy who looked to him for guidance and support.

How could all this please God?  How could English society demand this of him?  What had he done?

John Kenworthy's demons danced about him that night.  He felt that he had committed a rash act, but in fact, he had not.  His report to the constables had been anything but rash.  It had been thought out for weeks, planned and analyzed, scrutinized and debated in his mind.  He had sought the advice of a respected member of clergy who advised him that reporting this crime was not only warranted, but also obligatory.  He had also carefully weighed this edict against the words of Mrs. Hewitt who beseeched him to remain silent.  Never in his entire life had John engaged in such detailed and cautious consideration before taking an action, yet this was such a monumental and terrible action.  In turns, he regretted what he had done, then he justified it, and the cycle repeated.  Whether his decision to speak out was right or wrong truly didn't matter anymore.  The deed was done and could not be undone. He would have to carry it through to the end.

John did finally fall asleep, but he could not have slept much longer than an hour before Samuel was shaking him awake. "John, it's morning. It's time to get out of bed. Where were you so late last night? Oh, you won't tell me, but you must get up. We must get to the bookshop. We don't want to be sacked!"

After rising, washing, dressing and eating some bread and cheese, John said to Samuel, "Go to the shop and meet Mr. Medhurst in the street. Tell him that I am taken slightly ill and need some minutes, but that I will be around shortly. Then help him to remove the shutters, just as you usually help me." With that, Samuel was off. John left the room shortly after and met with Saunders at the locksmith shop. The keys duplicated, he hurried off to report to his job at the bookshop.

Meanwhile, Walter Boniface had risen, written in his dream log, performed his customary ablutions, eaten breakfast and descended the stairs. The process of shutter removal was slightly behind schedule, but not by long enough to cause any concern. He made a quick visual survey of the shop and found all in order. No more than a couple of minutes later than normal, Mr. Medhurst and Samuel entered. Noting John's absence, the bookseller asked, "Are we missing one of our own?"

Mr. Medhurst replied, "Samuel informs me that John is slightly ill and begs a few minutes, but that he expects to be around shortly."

Speaking directly to Samuel, the shop owner inquired, "It's nothing too serious, I hope?"

Samuel replied, "He truly didn't tell me, Sir. He's seemed out of sorts since Saturday last."

"Well, I'm sure we can get by without him for a short time." Walter resolved to inquire of the young man as to his wellbeing as soon as he arrived. "Now then Samuel, give the shop its morning sweeping."

No customers visited in the first twenty minutes of business and when John arrived, quite out of breath, Mr. Boniface took him aside. "Is everything alright, my boy. I've been told that you were a bit ill."

"I'm so sorry, Sir. I simply had a dizzy head this morning and needed a few minutes longer than usual. I shan't let it happen again."

"John, I don't care that you are a few minutes late on this one day. I'm only concerned that you are well. Samuel tells me that you have been acting unusual since Saturday. Do you need to discuss anything?"

"No sir," replied John curtly, "All is well." Although his employer was unconvinced, there was nothing he could do but to go on with the day.

The dearth of customers in the first few minutes was redeemed by a steady flow throughout the remainder of the day. John himself made several sales and earned a good commission. Mr. Boniface sold a rare book for twelve pounds, over six of that being profit, and Mr. Medhurst was busy as well. And Samuel, for the first time ever, sold a book in his own right to a young boy visiting the shop with his family. It was certainly not an expensive book, but it was a sale, nonetheless. He was granted commission of three farthings – a pittance, but it was the first money he had ever earned beyond his basic wages. Samuel and the two gentlemen were all in good spirits as they went upstairs for dinner. John, quite obviously, was not, but he shared the meal anyway.

The meal completed, John and Samuel descended the stairs. Once in the street, far enough away from the shop that they would not be heard, John scolded the younger boy. "Don't you be telling anyone about how I've been acting, like you did this morning. If I'm a bit out of sorts it doesn't concern you, and it doesn't concern Mr. Boniface either. Now, go back to our room, or wherever you want to go. I will be out late tonight."

"But John, what about our reading?" Samuel was visibly upset.

"Not tonight."  John then softened his tone as his *'older brother'* instinct reasserted itself.  "Go to our room for tonight.  We will read again to-morrow, or the next day."  With an annoyed look, Samuel walked on, and John proceeded to the place agreed upon the previous night to meet with the constables.  The two officers, Saunders and Jenkins were waiting for him.  All three returned to the street outside the bookshop and hid themselves in a secluded alley opposite.  For well over two hours, they watched the street where the bookshop was located.

There was no smoke from Mr. Medhurst's chimney pot.  As the sun set, it became apparent that there was a light in Mr. Boniface's parlour.  Movement could occasionally be seen at the window as one gentleman or the other rose to pour a glass of gin.  At one point, Jenkins suddenly jumped back when the figure at the window appeared to look in his di-rection, but he was quite sure that he had remained unseen.

Saunders, the senior constable, asked John if the men might be commit-ting the *'unnatural crime'* in the parlour, or in the adjacent bedroom.  John advised them that he thought this very unlikely as Mrs. Hewitt would be in her room directly behind, and he was sure that the men would not do anything of such a nature with her so close by.   He did not disclose the fact that Mrs. Hewitt was aware of their guarded secret.  He judged this information to be irrelevant to the matter at hand.

"Makes sense," Saunders agreed.  "Why else would the devils spend half of their nights in a single room over a cobbler if they could perform all their vile, unnatural deeds right there?"  After some period of watch-ing, Saunders asked John, "What time do these vermin usually come out and go up over the cobbler?"

John answered, based upon observations made during his nocturnal walks, "If they were going tonight, they would likely have already gone. I reckon they are staying in the parlour tonight."

They watched a while longer, then Saunders commented, "OK boys, I guess that's it for tonight.  We'll have to try again tomorrow.  These filthy dogs will have one more day.  Same instructions for tomorrow,

Master Kenworthy.  Do your job and meet us in the same place after your dinner."  With that, the two officers departed.

Despite his denunciation, John was annoyed by Saunders' vitriolic hatred for the two men.  He still held the view that these were two generally good people who had sinned before God, and that their anticipated arrest and subsequent atonement was the only way by which they may achieve salvation.  He knew that they would hang for their crime on Earth, but he truly believed that heaven awaited them thereafter.  He didn't appreciate them being referred to as *devils*, *vermin* or *filthy dogs*.


As all this was transpiring in the darkness outside, Walter and Albert were enjoying sips of gin and engaging in vivid conversation.  They briefly discussed their concerns about John, but then moved on to their habitual subject matter: dreams.

This evening, they spoke not of specific dreams read out from their logs, but rather of the purpose of dreaming in general.  Albert commented first on the subject, saying, "I am yet to be entirely convinced that dreams have any underlying meaning or offer any insight into our thoughts or personalities.  They seem silly, random visions conjured from the smoke of the day's events as distorted by our worries and cares."

Walter shook his head, "Oh Albert, you offered much the same opinion some months ago before you began telling me of your own dreams.  Since then, dreams have been a part of our discussions on nearly every evening.  We have sought meaning in both your dreams and mine.  Without doubt, we have been wrong in our interpretations at least as often as we have been correct, but in the very act of seeking meaning, we are developing theories as to the function of our minds.  Does this not give some underlying meaning, or at the very least, some purpose to the dreams?"

"Well, perhaps they do serve that purpose, but I doubt that The Creator put them in our heads with the sole intent that they become points of discussion." Although only lukewarm as to the Roman Catholic faith, Albert firmly believed, as did most people, in some sort of divine creator, even if he sometimes questioned whether this creator took any active interest in the world that he had created. He could not conceive of the diversity of the world arising without an intelligent designer.

"Yet dreams are in our heads, nonetheless," observed Walter. "For whatever reason, a creator, or a force of nature, seems to have put them there. Albert, I have thought much on the question of where and how dreams arise." Walter leaned toward his friend. "I have developed a broad interpretation of the workings of the mind through observation, and to be sure, through no small measure of conjecture. By my interpretation, I believe that there exists a part of the mind that might be termed a *watchman.* This watchman's duty is to regulate, or perhaps filter the thoughts which are perceived by our outward selves, and to separate these from the random, nonsensical ramblings of the remainder of the mind. I suppose that when we sleep, when we are quite tired, or even when we have had a bit too much gin, this watchman fails to effectively perform his duties. He allows random and unfiltered thoughts to be perceived. In spite of their bizarre and impossible nature, these are unvetted thoughts are often accepted as reality, in the moment of their perception at least."

Albert pondered this suggestion for a few moments. "This is a grand idea. You suggest that dreams are akin to burglars, thieves in the night unsatisfactorily repelled by an inept guard."

Walter, detecting that his friend was being playfully obstinate, explained, "That is not precisely what I meant, but I suppose it could be looked at that way. These burglars, however, steal nothing, but rather perform comedies and farces for us as we sleep. Of course, they occasionally perform plays of a most sinister nature, plays that no one would pay to watch in a theatre, but of which we often find ourselves captive

audiences in our sleep.  And we are temporarily gullible enough to accept these farces and horrors as reality."

"Well, that is a grand theory," commented Albert, he took a sip of gin,
then paused and took another.  Finally, he offered, "But Walter, you
speak of thoughts.  Even awake, I have known random thoughts, yet
they are just that, thoughts and nothing more.  Dreams have visions as
well.  How do you account for our ability to see dreams, as opposed to
simply thinking random thoughts?"

"Are visions and thoughts so very different, Albert?  Close your eyes and
think of my face.  Do you not see it in your mind?  And when you do see
my face, even among the countless thousands in London, you know at
once that it is me.  Must you not hold a vision of my face in your mind
when we are apart so that you might recognize me when we meet
again?  The same may be said for some many dozens of people who you
know and recognize at a glance.  Furthermore, in your dreams, are your
visions of faces and locations often accurate?  I think not, but the nap-
ping watchman fails to alert us to the inaccuracy."

At this moment, Walter stood to refill the glasses.  Glancing out of the
window, he thought he saw, for just a moment, some movement in the
moonlit street.  It looked, perhaps, as if it were a man beside the dis-
used shop across the road.  He pressed his face to the window for a
closer look, but whatever he had seen was gone, having receded into
the complete shadow of the alley.  Perhaps it was only a stray dog.  Albert, his back turned, didn't even notice his friend's moment of concern.

Albert generally understood Walter's views on the mental mechanics of
dreaming, even if he didn't fully agree.  He would give it some further
thought, but for the moment, he decided upon a minor change of subject.  "Walter, your very fine arguments have not spoken completely to
my original statement.  While you have suggested some possible mech-
anism by which dreams occur, you have said nothing of your views on
why they occur."

"I haven't any clue as to why dreams occur, but I accept that whoever or whatever created the mind would not have caused them to occur without reason.  Dreams must make us better in some way, elsewise dreaming would never have arisen.  Perhaps someday, when our men of science fully understand how the mind works, we might be able to answer the question of precisely why we dream but for now, it is a mystery."

"Do you think that anyone will ever fully understand the functioning of the mind, and thereby the reasons for dreams?  Is it within the capabilities of humanity to do so?"  Albert asked the question in a tone that made it clear that he was doubtful of even the possibility of a full understanding of the human mind.

"I think the concept not beyond the capabilities of human understanding, any more than it is beyond the collective capability of humans to travel to the moon.  Yet, I think that even two-hundred years from now, we shall likely still be engaged in the effort."

With that, the two gentlemen decided that it was time to end their evening.  Albert said softly to his friend, "Will you be my guest at my room tomorrow night, where we may tend our own fires."  Walter agreed and Albert walked back to his room.


When John Kenworthy arrived home at Shelton Street, he found Samuel still up and visually worried.  "What's going on, John?  You've been acting strangely."

"Don't worry about it, Samuel," he replied.  "I just had to visit with someone on my way home tonight."

Samuel looked at him and cocked his head to one side.  "John, have you been with a girl?"

John was a bit surprised, and even a bit amused, over young Samuel's guess.  The boy was also not entirely off the mark.  John had spoken to a young lady by the name of Elanor at church the previous Sunday, and for several Sundays before that.  Samuel had undoubtedly noticed.  He was working up the courage to ask her to join him for a walk in Regent's Park after church on some Sunday afternoon to come.  But Elanor was not the reason that John was late this night.  Flashing Samuel a genuine smile, he said, "No, there is not a girl.  Now go to sleep.  Tomorrow should be another busy day."

## Chapter 15 – A Family Broken

ohn slept intermittently that night, his mind a jumble of anger, sorrow, guilt, pride and confusion.  When dawn broke, he and Samuel prepared for yet another day at the bookshop.  John played his part, made a sale or two and acted, to the best of his ability, as if nothing were wrong.  However, when dinner time came, he politely excused himself.  On that evening, he could not bear to break bread with the men he was trying to apprehend for the commission of a capital crime.  Instead, he walked somewhat aimlessly in the area around Westminster Abbey and the nearby Houses of Parliament until it was time to meet with the constables.

At the wooden table in the kitchen over the bookshop, Samuel wondered at the empty chair.  He was most fortunate to be blissfully unaware of the secrets that surrounded him.  He was unaware of the horrible danger that Messrs. Boniface and Medhurst faced.  He was unaware of the absent John's tortuous inner turmoil, and the awful act that it had led him to.  He was also unaware that this would be his final dinner at that table.  He thought that his newfound *'family'* would nurture and care for him for countless days to come, and, with the exception of John, that family thought the same.

Dinner completed, Samuel helped Mrs. Hewitt to clean up, then left the kitchen and headed to Shelton Street.  Walter and Albert gathered their hats and coats, wished the housekeeper a good evening, then descended the stairs and walked the short distance to the little door beside the cobbler shop.  They ascended the stairs to Albert's room, locked the door and latched it with the newly installed bolt.

John and two constables took up position in the shadows across the street.  After quite some time, Saunders, the senior officer, advised that the moment had come for him to move inside.  Taking the larger of his duplicate keys, he opened the door from the street and quietly crept up the stairs.  Jenkins remained in the street, walking nonchalantly about, awaiting a signal from his superior.  John was ordered to stay out of sight in the shadows.

Saunders crouched, ear to the door of Mr. Medhurst's room.  He was listening for sounds that might indicate the correct moment to invade.  Ever so slowly, silently, he placed the smaller key in the lock and turned it.  Thanks to the newly installed bolt, the door did not move.  Oh, how that bolt, if installed at an earlier date, could have prevented this entire nightmare.  Saunders waited there, listening patiently for any sign that the time was right to make his move.  When he thought the moment correct, the senior constable used his considerable bulk to smash through the door, ripping the sliding bolt from the frame.

Saunders had his quarry.  Two men, until that moment lying together, jumped up in a state of shock and horror.  Jenkins rushed up the stairs.  The briefest of struggles ensued, after which one constable was in control of each man.  An examination was performed showing that there had been emission.  The raid was a success.  Everything had gone to plan, and the deed was done.

After being given a moment to don shirt and trousers, Walter Boniface and Albert Medhurst were handcuffed and led down the stairs.  As previously arranged, John met with them outside so that he might positively identify them to the officers.  "Are these the men you reported to us, Master Kenworthy?"  John nodded his head, trying to avoid eye contact but unable to look away.

Upon seeing John, Mr. Medhurst became enraged.  "You devil.  You despicable ingrate!  What have you done!  You Monster!"  Mr. Boniface, on the other hand, flashed a look of profound disappointment, but said nothing.  This glance hurt John far worse than Mr. Medhurst's insults.

John was commanded to come to the police office the next day to make formal statements.  Walter Boniface and Albert Medhurst were hauled away, and the scene was cleared leaving the street dark and silent.  John slowly wandered off.  As he walked past the shuttered bookshop, now his former place of employment, he thought of all that was now lost, and he walked on.  He varied his usual route to Shelton Street so that he passed the church where he worshiped on Sundays.  He truly believed that he had done what God wanted him to do.  From outside the gate, he said a small prayer of thanks for the strength that he had been given that evening, then he went home to his room.

Samuel, still blissfully unaware of anything being amiss, quizzed him again on the reason for his lateness.  Once again, John did not answer.  He knew that the childish ignorance that Samuel had enjoyed had also come to an end, but that could wait until the morning.

Walter Boniface was forcibly shoved into a cell with many rough-looking men.  A short distance away, Albert Medhurst was shoved into a similar cell.  Both were terrified.  Both knew that all was lost.  There was no hope.  They had long known that this might happen should their secret ever be revealed.  They had even discussed the possibility over gin once or twice.  Now that this worst fear had become reality, there was nothing to do but to accept the outcome.

The next morning, each was interviewed separately by the magistrate, Lord Stephenson.  Walter Boniface had little to say and was fully resigned to his fate.  Albert was more enraged and animated, and more willing to grasp at straws.  He spoke some untruths, both out of fear and anger.  Albert was aware that Walter had undertaken significant expenses some months earlier on John's behalf, both for medical bills and for legal counsel.  The judge at John's trial had confirmed Walter's right to pursue this money via a civil suit.  Albert claimed that John had demanded a letter confirming that his employer would not pursue this matter and that he had threatened, if he did not receive this letter, that he would expose them.  This was untrue, and almost immediately, Albert wished that he hadn't said it.  However, he was never given an opportunity to retract his accusation.

As the first light of dawn penetrated the grime on their window, Samuel was out of bed and getting ready for what he thought would be another routine day at the bookshop.  The time had come for John to break the news.  "Samuel," John said, "Sit down for a moment."  Samuel sat on the edge of his bed and John pulled up a crude wooden chair in front of him.  "I'm afraid we will need to look for new employment as we will no longer be working for Mr. Boniface."

Shocked and confused, Samuel simply stammered out the question, "But, why?"

"Mr. Boniface and Mr. Medhurst were both taken into custody last night.  They are now in prison."

"In prison!  Why are they in prison?"

"Samuel, they are sodomites."  The young boy, having recently spent three months in a squalid and violent prison himself, was completely familiar with that term.

"Oh," said Samuel, perhaps with some surprise, but not appearing to be repulsed by the revelation.  "How did they get found out?"

John explained, "I found out by accident, and after discussing the matter with the Reverend Mr. Hillyard, I felt it was required, by God, that I report this crime to the authorities."

"You?  You betrayed them, John?"  Tears welled up in the boy's eyes, then he began pounding his fists against John's shoulders and chest, screaming, "How could you do that!  They were both so good to us!"

John allowed himself to receive the boy's blows for a few moments.  After a short time, Samuel, still enraged, jumped up from the edge of his bed.  He slipped his feet into his shoes, leaving the laces untied, and he did not take the time to put on his hat.  "Samuel, wait…" called John, but it was to no avail.   The boy ran out of the room, down the stairs and into the street below.

Samuel ran to the bookshop, desperately hoping that it was all a cruel joke.  When he arrived, he saw an unfamiliar man exiting from the stairway door that led to the first floor.  Moments later, he saw Mrs. Hewitt exiting via the same door.  She was angry and appeared to be crying.  Samuel continued to watch for a few more minutes.  Someone had forcibly removed the shutter that had secured the shop door and rough-looking men were going in and out.  By this time, Mr. Medhurst should have been walking along the street on his way to the store, but he was not.  After some minutes of watching from a distance, Samuel ran to Mrs. Hewitt, who took him in her arms.  "Oh, dear boy, John has done a terrible thing."

"It's true then," sobbed Samuel.  "He told me what he did, but I wasn't sure if he was telling a cruel joke."

"He has condemned the two kindest men in all the world."  Mrs. Hewitt was beside herself.

 An officious-looking individual who had stepped out of a carriage a couple of minutes earlier walked over to Mrs. Hewitt.  He identified himself as a court official and gave his name which was immediately forgotten.  "Are you Walter Boniface's housekeeper then?"

"Yes… I am."  Mrs. Hewitt was still crying uncontrollably.

The court official spoke coldly, "This building, as the property of an accused sodomite, is being seized in the name of The Crown.  If you have any personal belongings inside, you may retrieve them, but be sure to check with me before you take anything away.  Do be smart about it, as we will be sealing the door in only a moment."

"Oh Samuel, this is horrible.  Come with me to help me move my belongings."  Samuel and Mrs. Hewitt made one final trip up the very familiar stairs.  They walked past the wooden table in the kitchen where so many delicious meals had been enjoyed as a group.  This group was as close to a true family as the boy had ever known.  Samuel waited while Mrs. Hewitt packed a large bag, and a smaller one.  She also retrieved a bundle that had been tucked beneath her mattress.  This contained a few pounds in silver and small bank notes that she had saved over the years.

With Samuel's assistance, Mrs. Hewitt brought her small load of luggage out to the street where it passed inspection by the court officer.  He asked her, "Do you know the address where you will be staying."  Mrs. Hewitt stated that she didn't know.  "Well, do advise the nearest police office once you do know.  We should like to keep account of where we might find you as your testimony may be required in front of the court."  There and then, she resolved not to comply with this request.

The two former employees of Walter Boniface walked away from the bookshop for the last time.  Samuel asked, "Where will you go, Mrs. Hewitt?"

"For the moment, Samuel, I suppose I will go to stay with my sister in Woolwich.  Perhaps I will seek work in that area.  I always thought that I would grow old housekeeping for Mr. Boniface."

Samuel looked at her with a sombre expression.  "They will be hanged, won't they?"

A new flood of tears gushed forward from Mrs. Hewitt's eyes as she answered, "Oh Samuel, they will almost certainly be hanged."  The two, carrying the housekeeper's scant baggage, had walked in a daze for a couple of blocks before either realized that they had no plans regarding their immediate destination.  Mrs. Hewitt asked, confused, "Oh, my boy, but where are we going right now?"  Samuel considered his room at Shelton Street, but that was also John's room.  He did not want to face John, and he knew that Mrs. Hewitt would feel the same way.  As a boy of limited means, he had no alternative suggestion to offer.  After several minutes, Mrs. Hewitt answered her own question.  "Samuel, come with me to my sister's home in Woolwich.  I am certain that she would be willing to accommodate both of us for a short time, and we can both seek out new employment."

"I would like that very much," replied Samuel.  "But before we leave, I do need to go back to my room one last time.  I need to get my hat, and my other shirt, and…"

"I understand," Mrs. Hewitt said.  "Let's go there now, but if we encounter John we will leave at once and return at another time when he is not present.  My nerves could not endure a meeting with him."


In the Shelton Street room, John was sitting and thinking.  In the midst of his uncertainty about what he had done, he did harbour one unambiguous regret.  He deeply regretted the harm that his action had caused to Samuel.  He did not intend to stay in that room, but Samuel did not have enough money to pay the rent on his own, even for a short time.

Thanks to his burgeoning skill as a young bookseller, John had managed to save a significant amount of money over the last several months.  He decided to give a portion of those savings to Samuel while still retaining enough for his own immediate needs.  He would leave that room, and he would leave London, forever.  He wrote a letter to the younger boy.  He then placed that letter in a bundle that contained a few small bank notes and a bit of silver coin.  He also included in the bundle the old bible that he had been using to help Samuel study both reading and religion.

John next packed his few personal belongings into a very old case (that had once belonged to the now hanged James).  He stepped outside of the room, locked the door then slid his key beneath it.  As for the keys to the bookshop and to Mr. Medhurst's room over the cobbler shop, he tossed these in a trash heap outside.  John walked away down the dirty Street.  As crowded as ever, the street nonetheless seemed lonely on that day.


Some minutes before John's departure, Samuel and Mrs. Hewitt had arrived at Shelton Street.  Mrs. Hewitt waited outside while Samuel went to the door of his room.  John could be heard inside.  He was making quite a lot of noise indeed.  Samuel was concerned that he might be doing some mischief, but he did not have the nerve to enter.  He left and returned to the street.  Watching from a discrete distance, he and Mrs. Hewitt saw John leaving, rough case in tow, about a quarter of an hour later.

Samuel seized this opportunity to retrieve his belongings from the room.  Upon entering, he noticed a small bundle on his own bed.  His name had been written on it.  He opened it to find the tattered old bible, some paper bank notes, some coins and a letter which read:

> *Dear Samuel:*
>
> *I did only what the laws of God and men said that I must do.  This money is some of what I have earned in commissions at the bookshop.  I give it to you, along with our bible.  The money will pay the rent on this room for some time, or you may do something else with it.  I shall not be coming back.  I am not sorry for what I have done, but I am sorry that it has hurt you.  Goodbye, and may God bless you.*
>
> *John.*

In all, the bundle contained eight pounds in bank notes, and nearly another two in silver.  Samuel accepted the money, although it did nothing to quell his anger.  He initially threw the letter to the floor, that being the amount of respect he felt it deserved.  Afterwards, he thought better of this action.  He was wise enough to know that a young boy with significant amounts of money might arouse suspicion.  He picked up the letter and put it in his pocket to serve as confirmation of his ownership of the bank notes, should the question ever arise.  He left the bible laying on the bed when he turned to leave the room.

Nearly all of John's belongings had been removed and as Samuel was leaving, he noticed the key on the floor near to the door.  He correctly deduced that John had slid it under the door after he had locked up.  He wondered for a moment where John might be going.  Quickly, however, he realized that he didn't much care.  He picked up the key and took it, along with his own, to the landlord on the ground floor, advising him that the room was no longer required.  He then left the building for the final time.

Samuel rejoined Mrs. Hewitt in the street.  He said to her, "I have money.  How do we get to Woolwich?"

John Kenworthy was quite sincere in his letter to Samuel.  He never intended to return to the room in Shelton Street.  He had long dreamt of leaving the great city altogether and in light of recent events, he felt that now was the most appropriate time to depart.  He had heard of places in the south of England, like Brighton or Eastbourne, where wealthy people travelled to enjoy the seaside or bathe in the surf.  He was certain that he could find work in such a place.  Without doubt, there would be employment in a shop or an inn for someone such as himself.  Furthermore, he had retained enough money to pay for the most inexpensive form of transportation to such a location, and for basic bed and board for a week or so, until he found such a situation.

There was another reason that John had his eyes set upon the south.  He had never seen the ocean.  To live in England, a nation surrounded by the sea, yet having never seen it seemed unjust to him.  He was certain that he could find some short moment, when the gentry were looking the other way, that he might step into the ocean and feel the cool salt water on his skin.  At the very least, the clean, clear wind blowing in from almost endless seas would be a welcome change from the great city's filthy fog and continual stench.  John had just one final duty left to perform before his departure from London.  He headed to the police office to give his formal statement regarding Mr. Boniface and Mr. Medhurst.

Mrs. Hewitt flagged down a cab, a new experience for her.  To catch a stagecoach to Woolwich, she and Samuel would need to go to an inn known as The Spread Eagle in Gracechurch Street.  On her several previous journeys, Mrs. Hewitt had walked from the bookshop, unless she could find a ride with a friendly merchant or carter in exchange for a few pennies.  In this case, with a load of both her luggage and Samuel's, and with some cash on hand, a cab seemed the most reasonable way to make the journey.

Upon arrival at Gracechurch Street in the late morning, the two travellers were told that a coach would be departing at two o'clock in the afternoon.  They purchased tea and some cold beef and waited.  The coach departed at the advertised time, crossed London Bridge and proceeded eastward.

Almost immediately, Samuel was further from his place of birth than he had ever travelled before.  He might have thought this journey to be a great adventure, were not the circumstances so dire.  Homes and warehouses, factories and parks streamed past, but they were all blurred by the horror of the day and by the magnitude of what had been lost.  The last several months had been truly wonderful for Samuel and he had dared to imagine that this would continue indefinitely.  Yet now, on this one terrible day, all was lost; his home, his livelihood and save for Mrs. Hewitt, all of those he viewed as family.

Some riders left, and joined the coach at Deptford, and some more at Greenwich.  Finally, the coach stopped in front of a very unpromising inn in Woolwich.  Mrs. Hewitt and Samuel were left alone on a roadside, no one else having disembarked at this location.  They found themselves in a place that made Shelton Street look posh by comparison.  "We'd best be going, Samuel."

After walking a short distance to the south, away from the Thames, they arrived at a narrow street lined with shops.  Mrs. Hewitt paused in front of a somewhat poor-looking bakery.  She peered through the dusty window for a moment, apparently scanning the interior for the presence, or absence, of some unknown thing.  A woman looking a good deal older than Mrs. Hewitt was inside the bakery, toiling at the task of kneading dough.  As the pair stepped through the door, this woman's face, at first set in a scowl, quickly turned to a look of delighted astonishment.  "Elizabeth," said the woman, "What an unexpected surprise!"

"Caroline, it is so good to see you."  Mrs. Hewitt introduced Samuel to her sister, then explained, "We both find ourselves very suddenly out of work and had nowhere else to turn."

"Oh, my dear Elizabeth, what has happened?"

Mrs. Hewitt explained that it was most complicated, and that Mr. Boniface had suffered a serious run-in with the law.  She did not specifically state the nature of his alleged crime.  "We only ask for shelter for a couple of nights, after which we will make arrangements for ourselves.  We do have money to cover expenses."

"Well of course you are most welcome," responded Caroline.  "You do know, however, that *he* will not be especially welcoming."  Mrs. Hewitt's sister was referring to William Wilkens, her husband and, in theory at least, a baker.  He did far less baking than drinking, leaving most of the work to his wife and their sons, Robert and Stephen.

"I have always been able to tolerate him before, Caroline.  I shall do so again."  Even to young Samuel, it was obvious by her tone that Mrs. Hewitt harboured a serious dislike for William Wilkens, and that her sister was very much aware of this opinion.

Back in central London, John underwent a lengthy interrogation by Lord Stephenson.  The magistrate asked many times who the two *'mollies'* interacted with, both during and after business hours.  Just as many times, John assured his interrogator that he knew of no personal interactions with anyone and that the only people he had ever seen either speak to were those on business at the shop.  The magistrate was keenly interested in the men's relationship with John.  Had he taken part in any of their *'unnatural crimes?'*  Had he been asked to do so?  Had Samuel?  John was becoming increasingly exasperated by the line of questioning.  Finally, Lord Stephenson asked, "If these two have been as good to you as you say, then why did you report their crime?  If you had such a good situation, then why did you destroy it, and condemn them both to their deaths?"

"I was required to do so by the laws of God and men," was John's well-practiced answer.

For the first time, the magistrate looked directly into John's eyes.  He seemed to peer into John's very soul, albeit only for a moment.  He didn't reveal what he saw but simply riffled through some papers on his desk.  After an awkward pause, he said, "I see in these records that you had your own trouble with the law some months ago.  You were charged with murder and highway robbery but acquitted.  You admitted that you planned to steal from Walter Boniface and that you recruited the other boys to aid you.  You killed one of those boys during the robbery.  You were very fortunate not to hang for that crime."

"My lord, I confessed my guilt to the degree that I was guilty, and I paid a penalty of three months confinement in prison."

The magistrate, reading the court record from the trial, continued, "It also says here that Walter Boniface was your most ardent defender.  Additionally, I see that the justice in that case cautioned you that he had the right to launch a civil matter against you to recover expenses for doctor's accounts, and for your legal counsel."

"If you please, Sir, I do know what the record says as I was there."  John was anxious to get out of that office.  He was thinking of ocean waves breaking on the beach in some seaside town, and he wanted to depart for that town as quickly as possible.  London, where he had spent his entire life, now seemed stifling and confined.  The sooner he could leave it, the happier he would be.

The magistrate continued, "You likely also know that should he be convicted of sodomy, all debts owed to Walter Boniface are cancelled."

"I did not know that My Lord."

"Didn't you?" continued the magistrate.  "I have been told otherwise.  I interviewed Messrs. Boniface and Medhurst earlier this morning.  I was told that you did know of this fact, and that you threatened their exposure if Mr. Boniface failed to provide you with a letter stating that he would not pursue this civil matter."

"Sir, that is entirely untrue.  I absolutely cannot believe that Mr. Boniface would say that about me."

"He didn't," replied the magistrate.  "Walter Boniface, for some reason, still seems to care about you.  Albert Medhurst, however, gave you up entirely."

"No, Sir.  He is lying.  He is just trying to save himself.  I never did such a thing."  John had become seriously concerned.

Lord Stephenson replied, "Albert Medhurst was caught by two officers from the magistrate's court in the commission of an act of sodomy.  He cannot save himself and he is aware of this.  Yet he can still testify against you.  He has accused you of extortion, saying that you told him to convince Mr. Boniface to produce this letter, otherwise you would expose both of them."  The magistrate stood and wandered around the room.  "True, this might be simply a case of vengeance, but it does seem odd that you, a convicted criminal, would be so bound to the laws of God that you were inclined to sacrifice steady employment offered by

Mr. Boniface, not to mention a meal cooked each evening by his servant, all to satisfy your supposedly pristine sense of morality.  I simply do not believe it.  John Kenworth, you must now consider yourself in custody on suspicion of the crime of extortion."

A short time later, John found himself in a place that he had vowed never to see again.  He was in a prison cell.  He thought that he would be on his way to Brighton that very afternoon, dipping his feet into the ocean a day or two later.  Instead, he was incarcerated once again, and Mr. Boniface would not be coming to his rescue this time.

In Woolwich, Mrs. Hewitt's nephews, Robert and Stephen, returned from their errands.  They were left in charge of the bakery for a short time while their mother escorted Mrs. Hewitt and Samuel to the flat above.  William Wilkens, recumbent in the flat at the time, noted their arrival.  "Ahh, blessed with another visit, are we Elizabeth.  And what's this?  Another mouth to feed I suppose?"

"William," said Mrs. Hewitt coldly, "This is Samuel.  He worked for Mr. Boniface along with me.  Samuel, this is my brother-in-law, Mr. William Wilkens."

Samuel bowed deeply and said, "Pleased to meet you Sir."  In truth, he was not.

Mr. Wilkens barked, "He will not eat a morsel of food that is not paid for.  Do you hear me, not a morsel!"  The nominal baker then went back to his bottle of rum and stopped noticing the new arrivals.

The time for dinner drawing near, Samuel and Mrs. Hewitt visited a local butcher to obtain some additional pork for a stew, already simmering, which would need to fill more bellies than expected.  Samuel looked out for any local business which might be in need of assistance.  He was told that the undertaker was looking for a boy to assist in his trade.  When that blonde-haired boy with a face that positively beamed sunshine inquired as to the job, the undertaker actually laughed, a rare sight to be sure.  Samuel would look further for work in the morning.

Dinner at Mr. Wilkens' table was a sombre affair.  It was clear that no one was permitted to speak unless in direct response to a question posed by Mr. Wilkens, but that individual posed no questions.  The meal was passed in silence.  Afterwards, a rough blanket was provided to Samuel who made his bed on the floor at the foot of those belonging to the two Wilkens boys.

Stephen was the younger of these boys, but still at least three years older than Samuel.  Robert was a year or two older yet.  As they turned in for the night, one of them asked, "So, what was your employer arrested for?"  Samuel refused to say.  They pressed, but he never budged.

That night, Samuel dreamt of Walter Boniface and Albert Medhurst.  He dreamt of the wonderful warm friendship that they had shown at their dinner table, so unlike the one he had just experienced.  He remembered in his dreams the sense of excitement that he felt every morning as he removed the shutters, eager to face the day and find out what surprises it may have in store.  He dreamt that he was once again honing his reading skills under John's tutelage, (although this particular dream ended with John bursting into flames).  He dreamt of all that was now lost.

Some strange and misguided sense of justice had taken hold of John and he had done the unthinkable.  Samuel had lost every friend he had, save only for Mrs. Hewitt.  He did not cry, but the corners of his eyes each held a small tear as he pondered a future, once thought to be secure, but now rife with uncertainty.

While Samuel's bed on the floor was less than comfortable, John's sleeping arrangements in the cells of the Magistrate's Court were even more unpleasant.  Strangely though, his dreams were very similar to

Samuel's.  He saw in his nighttime imagery all that he had thrown away.
He desperately wanted to believe that his betrayal had saved not only
his own soul, but that of Mr. Boniface as well.  He willed himself to believe this, suppressing all those voices of doubt that welled up in his
mind.  He was angry with Mr. Medhurst for his lies and was saddened
that this individual might be throwing away his chance at redemption.
But then again, Albert Medhurst was a Roman Catholic, a papist.  Perhaps they could not be redeemed.  Nevertheless, John had not forgotten the years of kindness shown to him by that gentleman.  He could
certainly forgive Mr. Medhurst some lies spoken out of anger and desperation, and he hoped that God could forgive the error of his faith.

The following day, John was permitted a visit by clergy.  A young
preacher spoke to him, and John poured out his heart about the advice
given by the Reverend Mr. Hillyard, the turmoil that it had aroused
within him, and how it had led to the decision to betray the most generous man in the world.  The young and inexperienced preacher was overwhelmed, completely at a loss as to how he should respond, so he decided to send a message to the Reverend Mr. Hillyard seeking advice.
To the surprise of both, the far more experienced pastor came to visit
that very afternoon.  "Oh, my young man," he said to John, "I know that
times are hard right now, but you did the right thing.  When you spoke
to me those weeks ago, I did not imagine that the sin of which you al-
luded was so great.  In earlier times, The Almighty destroyed entire cities for such crimes and that they should still occur in this modern day is
a shameful stain on humanity.  And now one of them compounds his sin
with lies toward you, and I am told that he is a papist as well.  There is
but little hope for his soul, but the other, Walter Boniface, I think he
might be saved if he fully repents and falls upon his knees before God.  I
will go to him personally and pray with him, for no matter how vile, he
can be forgiven by The One who can forgive all."

John, for the first time, realized that the advice given by this man of God
was the primary motivation that finally convinced him to betray his ben-
efactor.  The unusual, yet wonderfully inclusive family group of which he

had been a part was now destroyed, scattered to the winds.  Were the advice of this man different, John would look forward each morning to arriving at the bookshop with Samuel, removing the shutters, selling books for commission, eating delicious home-cooked meals and retiring to the room in Shelton Street where he would read with young Samuel.  Furthermore, two honest and generous gentlemen would be sharing their kindness with the world, and their love with one another, instead of facing their inevitable executions.  "Reverend," inquired John, "How can you be certain that God disapproves of sodomy."

"My boy, it is written in The Bible.  *'If a man also lie with mankind, as he lieth with a woman, both of them have committed an abomination: they shall surely be put to death;'*"

"And how do you know that the bible is correct?  Could it not be wrong?"

The reverend, clearly taken aback, responded, "Take care, young man, for your words are perilously close to blasphemy.  The Bible is the inspired word of God.  It sets the foundation of our faith, and of our belief in The Saviour.  We are a people of The Book.  Sodomy is known to the whole world to be among the most heinous of sins, the vilest of crimes.  Those who commit such a crime are scoundrels of the most despicable kind and must suffer the most extreme punishment here upon earth, yet, I think and believe, that God will forgive Walter Boniface if he fully and unconditionally repents his horrid sins."

John looked directly into the preacher's eyes.  "Walter Boniface is not a despicable scoundrel.  He is the kindest man I ever knew, and your advice, based upon the bible which you hold so dear, convinced me to betray him.  Albert Medhurst is also a good man.  I say that even though he has made a false accusation against me.  He is angry for what I have done to him, and I forgive him this little wrong he has done to me.  You say that he cannot be saved simply because he is a papist.  He worships the same god, only in a manner which differs slightly from that of the Church of England.  How can you say that he cannot be saved? Truly,

Reverend, I do not reject Our Saviour, but I have no further use for the hateful edicts of the bible, or for your advice on these matters."

The reverend stood up, insulted. "I have rarely been spoken to in such a manner, and never by one so young! You had best take care for your own soul, young man."

John cared little that the preacher had taken offense. He simply said, "I suggest that you do not speak with Mr. Boniface, unless it is to apologize to him. I am ashamed to admit that even if given the opportunity, I would not have the strength to face him for the purpose of offering my own apology."

"I will take my leave now," said the preacher, the annoyance in his voice apparent. "If you wish to speak again in the future and if you are able to comport yourself a more Christian manner, then I am still available to you." John would never see the Reverend Mr. Hillyard again.

A couple of hours later, a guard arrived and informed John of the magistrate's decision that he could be bailed for five pounds. He had just marginally more than that on his person and he walked out a free, yet completely broke, young man. There truly was only one place that he could go. Despite his promise to Samuel not to return, he walked back to Shelton Street. Upon arrival, he knocked on the door that had so recently been his own. Receiving no reply, he went to the landlord hoping to beg entry, but he was informed that the keys had been returned and the room was available to let. With only two shillings and a few pennies in his pocket, John had no means by which he might pay for this, or any other room. He slept rough that night. He would have been better off in prison.

In Woolwich, Samuel spent the day following his arrival searching for work of any kind. He was not successful. These were not his streets and this fact seemed obvious to the area's life-long residents. He would spend just one more night on the floor in that tiny bedroom and the next day, he would walk all the way back to central London.

Mrs. Hewitt hugged Samuel as he left.  In the twenty-two years that remained in her lifetime, she would not see him again.  They would, however, exchange letters in those ensuing years.  Mrs. Hewitt would write to Samuel, telling him of her work at the bakery alongside her sister and nephews, this being after the (untimely?) death of William Wilkens. Samuel would tell her about his newfound employment at a bookshop in Paternoster Row and how, many years later, he became a respected bookseller in his own right.  He would write to her about his marriage, and about his twin sons who he named Walter and Albert.  The final letter that Samuel would write to Mrs. Hewitt, just weeks before her peaceful death, would tell of the arrival of his youngest child; a daughter who he named Elizabeth.

## Chapter 16 – The Final Chapter

John was quickly acquitted on the charge of extortion and had his bail returned.  He was, however, informed that he would be compelled by law to appear as a witness at the sodomy trial of Walter Boniface and Albert Medhurst.  This trial was to take place during the September assizes, nearly three months hence.  To his dismay, he did not have nearly enough money to travel to the southern coast of England, then to return to London for the trial, and thereafter to return to the south.  He was compelled to remain in the dirty metropolis until that time, yet he had nowhere to call home.

John did some odd work during these months.  He earned a shilling here or two there, but without references and looking somewhat dishevelled, he found no long-term employment.  The small amount of money that he had retained was quickly exhausted.  He generally slept in the streets.  Once, when passing the workhouse at St. Martins in the Fields, John stopped by the gate.  Peering in at the sad gray ghosts of men, women and children in that place, he resolved that he would die before finding himself in such a situation.  He once saw Samuel carrying a heavy stack of books through St. Paul's Churchyard before disappearing into Paternoster Row.  He didn't make contact.  Samuel was better off without him, and he had not sunk so low that he failed to respect that fact.  He was genuinely gladdened to see that the young boy had found a new situation, and he wished him all the best.

The bookshop in Westminster, where John had spent such happy times, burned to the ground one night.  That place where he had felt as if he were a member of a family, the stacks of books that he had come to know so well, and the wooden table in the first-floor kitchen where he had enjoyed lovingly cooked meals were all reduced to ashes and cinders.  John had once dreamt of the shop's destruction by fire.  In that dream, he believed that he had ignited the flames.  In actuality, the culprit was another individual with a similarly warped sense of justice. This man was bent on cleansing the property of the stain he imagined to be left upon it through inhabitation by a sodomite.  He would eventually hang for his crime, as was the prescribed punishment for arsonists.

Even though John hadn't kindled the fire, it had, nonetheless, burned due to his actions.  His dream had come true.


After the long summer passed, the day of the trial finally arrived.  John cleaned himself up to the best of his ability, but in his torn and muddy clothes, this was to little avail.  He looked as much the vagabond as he had on that day when he had appeared in front of the bookshop, having just been released from prison.  Unfortunately, this time, Mrs. Hewitt was not there to help him make himself presentable.  He had betrayed her as well.

In his dishevelled state, John went to the court.  He was told to wait in a specified area until he was called.  When that call came, he listened to the two accused as they entered pleas of not guilty.  John was the first witness asked to speak.  He truthfully and accurately related the events of the night when he had taken the letter to the room over the cobbler shop.  He spoke in an unemotional monotone, his ability to express emotion having simply withered into nothingness.  He felt that he might be sick.  He looked at Walter Boniface and Albert Medhurst in the prisoner's box, each of them mere shells of the men that he remembered. On their faces, he did not see anger, but only deep disappointment.  He might have found expressions of anger easier to accept.  No mention was made of Mr. Medhurst's accusation of extortion against John.  It was a false charge, but an understandable one on the part of a man condemned by a broken promise.  His testimony complete, John was excused.

Constable Saunders, the senior officer involved in the arrest, gave a clinical account of his investigative procedure.  He gave credit to John who he said, by way of compliment, had been indispensable at bringing the prisoners to justice.  He told of holding his ear to the door of the room above the cobbler shop, waiting for telltale sounds.  He referred to his notebook as he described bursting through the door and witnessing the two men, still intimate.  He described all else.

The junior constable, Jenkins, testified next.  He described the same events from his point of view.

The judge then said, "The prisoners may now speak in their own defense."

Walter Boniface spoke.  His voice was hoarse and weak, almost unrecognizable.  He said, "My Lord, we compliment John Kenworth and the constables for telling the complete truth in this matter.  We have done the thing of which we are accused.  No lies have been spoken about us.  Yet who have we harmed?  We have stolen no property.  We have not wounded, nor have we killed anyone.  We have not put the security of the realm in peril, nor have we betrayed The King.  We are simply two people who dearly love one another, and we have expressed that love..."

"That will be quite enough!" the judge interrupted, forcefully.  "Are there any here to speak in the prisoners' defense?"  There was no one.  Turning to the jury, he continued, "The jury is cautioned that in returning a verdict of guilty, you will be condemning these two men to their deaths.  Therefore, you must only return such a verdict if you are certain, beyond all traces of doubt, that the accused are indeed guilty.  You may now deliberate."

The jury huddled briefly.  There was audible laughter from their direction.  In scarcely more than a minute, they turned back to the judge who asked, "Have you reached a verdict?"  He already had his black cap in his hand.

"We have, Your Lordship.  We find Walter Boniface guilty of sodomy.  We find Albert Medhurst guilty of sodomy.  We do not recommend mercy in either case."

Black cap on head, the judge dispassionately read out the sentence: "Walter Boniface, for the unnatural crime of sodomy, you are condemned to death by hanging. Albert Medhurst, for the same detestable crime, you are condemned to death by hanging. May God have mercy upon your souls. Those other unfortunate men condemned during this session to hang for crimes less vile than your own should feel repugnance if forced to share a scaffold with you. Consequently, you shall be executed separately, at an earlier date. Degraded as you are, let me exhort you to spend what little time you have left in this world in imploring forgiveness from that Being who is able and willing to extend mercy to the vilest sinner. The clerk will not enter any of the details of this trial into the official record."

And so it came to pass that case number 1220, heard at London's Criminal Court, commonly referred to as The Old Bailey, at the assizes of September 11th, 1822, was recorded as follows:

```
WALTER BONIFACE and ALBERT MEDHURST were
indicted for sodomy.

BONIFACE - GUILTY - DEATH.   Aged 42.
MEDHURST - GUILTY - DEATH.   Aged 32.

London Jury, before Mr. Justice Best.
```

And nothing more.

Walter and Albert were escorted to separate cells to await their common fate.


After leaving the courtroom, John Kenworthy walked. He walked without destination. He walked without purpose. He walked without thinking.

John experienced the streets as a drunkard might. He was only vaguely aware of their passing. He walked through The City in a weaving, purposeless path. He walked along Great Prescott Street, past the house where Doctor Paynter had once lived, the house he had visited on the fateful day when he first betrayed Walter Boniface.  Turning about abruptly, he walked past the Tower of London where those who betrayed The King had often spent their final days.  He walked on to St. Paul's Cathedral, that magnificent monument to faith in a god whose presumed wishes had convinced him to commit a monumental betrayal.  He realized, perhaps then or perhaps some time before, that this was a god in whose grace he had stopped believing.  He reversed his course once again and walked out onto London Bridge.  There, in one of the picturesque little alcoves lining the bridge, he sat and cried.

The scraps that remained of the young man once known as John Kenworthy sat in that alcove for a few minutes, or maybe it was an hour.  At last, he rose.  He walked to the very centre of the bridge, to the centre of the great arch.  He looked over the edge, down at the filthy River Thames.  The water was high but calm; it was slack tide.  Somehow, he would have preferred it to be rushing either in or out, but this would have to do.  He climbed onto the bridge parapet, and he flung himself into the murky water below.

Several people saw him jump.  Boats were sent out to effect a rescue, but there was no sign of him.  As the tide ebbed, the search moved further downstream, but it was still to no avail.  His body would be found three days later and some miles down river.  He was no longer in turmoil.


The discovery of John's body was deemed newsworthy enough to warrant two lines in the evening newspaper.  Having read this brief remark, one of the prison turnkeys called out to Walter Boniface in his dark cell, "Hey there, *molly*, you awake?  I just read about your boy there, called John Kenworthy.  You might be interested to know that he jumped off London Bridge right after your trial.  They just found his body, washed up at the Isle of Dogs.  Kind of me to tell ya, ain't it?"

It is a cruel irony that the turnkey probably thought that he was giving Walter a bit of good news, doing him some small favour.  He knew that John's report to the constables, and his testimony, were key to the discovery and conviction of the former bookseller.  He thought that his prisoner would be uplifted by the news; that he would view it as some measure of revenge for the fatal harms committed against him.  But the turnkey could not have been more wrong.  The sentence of death, Walter had accepted with stoic resolution, but this news made him cry like an infant.

The judge's welcomed promise of a quick end did not come to pass.  For two months, Walter and Albert languished in that cruel prison.  Both would have preferred to have the deed completed; to hang and be done with it.  Unlike a murderer or a robber who knows, in his heart, that he has done harm, these two gentlemen could not find any guilt within themselves.  The society in which they lived had simply decreed their nature to be abominable based upon the authority of ancient scripture.  Walter and Albert had not even guilt as companion in those dark cells.

At the end of those two seemingly interminable months, the final night came at last.  Walter Boniface lay on the hard wooden bench in his cold cell.  He was alone, hungry, uncomfortable and missing Albert.  The next day, he would be hanged.  He managed just a few moments of sleep and in those moments, he experienced one brief dream.  If he'd had access to his dream log, he would have recorded the single word, *Dreamt,*' to describe his very short unconscious vision.

What is it then; this supposed punishment that they call *Death*?  To kill is said to be a crime, but the state, in the name of The King, offers frequent public demonstrations of the practice for all to see.  Is that not a crime as well?  The church condones the killing of sinners in the name of God, but do they not also claim that all persons are created by the hand of God, in his perfect image?  Why does that God produce so many people who are so seriously flawed?  And why can he not correct his own errors, rather than leaving that task to those same seriously flawed humans?  If indeed God puts men and women upon the earth by divine will, then by what right do some few of these men decree that God's will should be overruled and that these persons should be removed from the Earth altogether?  Scripture, while enthusiastically condoning the killing of sinners and criminals, also renders the act absurd.


Walter Boniface was roughly dragged from his cell into the corridor.  A short distance away, Albert Medhurst was receiving the same treatment.  Their tormentors brought them close enough together that they were able to briefly speak; "We shall tend our own fires tonight, Albert," Walter said bravely.

"And for every night to come, Walter," was the equally courageous reply from his lover.

The two were led outside.  November's gloom had parted and although the air was cold, a bright sunshine pierced London's thick coal smoke.  The morning presented a vivid orange-yellow brilliance.  The gibbet stood close by, bathed in the glorious light of the morning.  The couple noted a pair of wooden stools thoughtfully placed beneath the nooses, clearly for their convenience.  They glanced toward one another.  Their eyes said goodbye.  Words were not needed.

Their hands were bound behind their backs.  They mounted their respective stools.  Hoods were placed over their heads, and all was darkness even in the bright sun.  Walter felt the rope being placed around his neck.  He heard the sounds of footsteps moving to and fro.  The cold November wind blew through his torn shirt, yet a hot sweat enveloped him.  Men, women, and children shouted at him.  He did not hear what they were saying.  It did not matter.

Suddenly, the stool beneath Walter's feet was forcefully removed.  The noose tightened around his neck, but the drop was so short that no catastrophic damage was done.  And there he hanged.  There was no fear.  He was aware of no pain.  In fact, he perceived a greater tranquillity than he had known in a very long time.  The crowds hooted and cheered in the distance, but they were of no concern.  This moment was his, and he would enjoy the peace of it.

In a final dream, dreamt while yet awake, Walter once again saw young John Kenworthy.  He could never hate that boy, no matter what calamities he may have wrought.  John was sitting with a shilling in his hand, beaming ear to ear with that boyish and endearing smile, as the cashbox gushed a fountain of money.  One final time, the young man reminded his former employer that one shilling was all he had ever wanted.

There was no time for yet another interpretation of this familiar vision, which Walter now welcomed as an old friend.  Dimmer, dimmer, the visions faded.  Walter's very last thought was of his beloved Albert, who he knew to be hanging beside him.  Dimmer still, then nothing.  Not sadness, not regret, not fear, not anger, not repentance, but simply nothing.  Nothing evermore.

*The End*

# Afterword

The excerpt from the records of The Old Bailey included in The Final Chapter is genuine, with only the names having been changed to match those of the characters in this book.  During the assizes of September 11th, 1822, before Mr. Justice Best, two men whose actual names were recorded as *John Holland* and *William King*, were sentenced to death for the crime of sodomy.  Their sentences were carried out in November of that same year.  It is to the memory of these two men, even if only in name, that I have dedicated this book.  I have timed its release to coincide with  the 200th anniversary of this trial.

In the epoch surrounding 1822, most records of the proceedings at The Old Bailey and other legal venues offer at least some small summary of the evidence presented in each case, often augmented by limited summaries of the testimony of witnesses and the prisoner's defence.  However, sodomy trials usually lack this information.  It was considered too distasteful to even record the scantest details of these trials.  These men were denied even an accusation in the official record.  The extremely brief record of the trial and sentence of John Holland and William King may be found at:

https://www.oldbaileyonline.org/browse.jsp?id=t18220911-76-off412&div=t18220911-76

This book has not been a biography of John Holland and William King. The narrative in this book has been entirely fictional, being only inspired by their fate.  Despite the lack of official records, some small amount of information regarding their trial can be found in newspaper articles of the time.  John Holland, for example, is reported to have had a wife and children.  The men's occupations are reported as being a bricklayer and a labourer, as opposed to booksellers.  We also cannot be certain as to the accuracy of these newspaper reports.  By way of example, William King is reported by various articles to have been of multiple different ages ranging from 32 to 60.

Another man, William North, was also convicted of sodomy at the same assizes, by the same judge, but the records suggest that his was likely a separate case.

It should also be noted that the term '*sodomy*' referred to any type of anal intercourse, be it between two men, a man and a woman, or a man and an animal.  The squeamishness of 19th century society regarding any of these acts generally means that no details are available.  A homosexual relationship between Holland and King is a presumption, but this is not absolutely confirmed by the scant records.

In this book, I have depicted the pair of booksellers as almost saintly figures.  Few, if any, human beings are quite as virtuous as my descriptions of William Boniface and Albert Medhurst.  However, even if a homosexual couple in that era did display such resplendent righteousness, it would have made no difference whatsoever in the outcome of their trial or their eventual fate.  In that time period, the revulsion that society felt toward the act of intercourse between two men was absolute.  As an illustration of this fact, consider this excerpt from a newspaper report referring to the sentencing of John Holland and William King, some parts of which I have borrowed as dialogue for the characters of Reverend Mr. Hillyard and the judge in the trial of Walter Boniface and Albert Medhurst:

> *"Silence being proclaimed, the RECORDER addressed*
> *the prisoners to the following effect:– "Prisoners, you*
> *have been convicted of a detestable crime during the*
> *present Session. – The Learned and excellent Judge*
> *who presided on your trial implored the Jury not to*

*return that verdict which must inevitably deprive you of life unless the evidence was conclusive beyond all doubt. That attentive and intelligent Jury have been forced, by the power of evidence and flash of truth, to come to that dreadful conclusion without hesitation; indeed, it was impossible they could have returned a different verdict. You have, by your abominations, disgraced human nature, and dishonoured the country in which you live. In the early ages of the world, the Almighty destroyed whole cities through the commission of crimes like yours; you have polluted the world, and must depart from it. — Those unfortunate men who have forfeited their lives, feel a repugnance to ascending the same scaffold with you, therefore the Court order that you be executed at an earlier and distinct period. Degraded as you are, let me exhort you to devote the little time you have to live, in imploring forgiveness of that Being who is able and willing to extend mercy to the violest sinner. It is my earnest wish that by your contrition, you may avoid that fire in an eternal world which consumed in former ages the inhabitants of whole cities, for a similar offence to yours."* — The Morning Post, September 25, 1822.[1]

For almost 200 years after their deaths, these two men were formally regarded as criminals having been justly executed under the law.  In

---

[1] Thanks to https://rictornorton.co.uk/ for posting newspaper excerpts regarding to this and many other cases related to homosexuality at various periods in history. — This quote retrieved April 5, 2022.  Citation: *Rictor Norton (Ed.), "Newspaper Reports, 1822", Homosexuality in Nineteenth-Century England: A Sourcebook, 29 December 2014, updated 6 June 2021 <http://rictornorton.co.uk/eighteen/1822new1.htm>.*

2016, at long last, The United Kingdom issued a pardon for all men convicted of homosexual relationships.  Commonly known as Turing's law after the famed WWII code breaker and pioneering computer scientist, Alan Turing, it wiped clean the convictions of about 15,000 living people, and posthumously overturned roughly 40,000 historic convictions, including those of John Holland and William King.

In several nations of the world, especially those ruled by authoritarian governments, be they under the control of religious or megalomaniacal rulers (the two are not mutually exclusive), execution remains the dictatorial response to versions of the expression of true love between consenting adults that some in power find objectional, like that between the fictional Walter Boniface and Albert Medhurst.

## Also by S. William Bennett

*Note that S. William Bennett was previously known simply as William Bennett (before a certain mega-corporation told him he couldn't use that name anymore for self-published books.)*

**In The Beginning** – *A secular and satirical reading of the best-selling book of all time.*

There's a certain old book lurking on the forgotten shelves of many of our homes. Most of us have at least a passing familiarity with a few of the more famous stories found within that book. The majority of us are aware of its tales of two naked people in a garden, of a big boat full of animals, and of the birth of a special baby. But only the odd person, scattered here and there, has actually read it cover to cover. *In The Beginning* is for people who really don't want to.

The central character is a being who exists outside of space and time as we perceive it, who is orders of magnitude more intelligent than any human, who is so different from us that we cannot even begin to imagine his greatness, and who configured our planet and our entire cosmos in just six days of epic creativity. He is known as Tom, and he is an irresponsible youth living in a star system known as Ko, in a parallel universe. Well, who did you think I was talking about?

The universe that Tom designs turns out far from perfect, but he does make an honest effort to do the right thing.  Sadly, he just can't seem to get any cooperation whatsoever from the dominant species on the one little planet that he decided to infuse with the miracle of life.

In The Beginning presents a satirical interpretation of the best-selling book in history, one which is just very, very slightly more plausible than the original.  It is a fictionalization of an ancient fiction.  Sometimes irreverent, sometimes willfully naïve, and sometimes just a bit serious, it strives to direct the thoughts of the reader on a course somewhat different from that plotted by priests and rabbis throughout the millennia.

***In the Beginning*** - https://www.amazon.com/dp/B014YSDD7U